Lock Down Publications and Ca$h
Presents

I0658342

QUEEN OF NAPTOWN

THE FIRST LADY

Written By
KEITH CHANDLER

First Edition 2025

Printed in the United States of America

This is a work of fiction. Names, characters, places, and incidents either
are products of the author's imagination or are used fictitiously. Any
similarity to actual events or locales or persons, living or dead, is
entirely coincidental.

Lock Down Publications
P.O. Box 944
Stockbridge, GA 30281
www.lockdownpublications.com

Like our page on Facebook: Lock Down Publications
www.facebook.com/lockdownpublications.ldp

Stay Connected with Us!

Text **LOCKDOWN** to 22828 to stay up-to-date with new releases, sneak peaks, contests and more…

Like our page on Facebook:
Lock Down Publications

Join Lock Down Publications/The New Era Reading Group

Visit our website:
www.lockdownpublications.com

Follow us on Instagram:
Lock Down Publications

Email Us: We want to hear from you!

Dedication

This book is dedicated to all that supported me along the way. Thanks to my family.

Chapter 1

The last memory of my father was when he prepared chicken, rice and mixed vegetables for dinner; and he bought out a bottle of wine.

"What's wrong," Black Jesus asked, as he noticed the disturbed look on his daughter Queen's face. She didn't respond. "Tell me what's wrong, don't ignore me and don't lie."

"I feel like something is going to go wrong when you leave daddy," Queen said looking down at her plate.

"Yeah, why don't you stay in tonight baby?" Kenya said rubbing the back of Black Jesus hand.

"Queen, you know I'm going to be good and Kenya, you know I have to make my moves," Black Jesus said standing to leave.

"We love you," Kenya said.

"You know I love the both of y'all too," Black Jesus said before walking out the front door.

Queen ran to the front window and watched her dad hop into his Audi truck and ride off. That was the last memory of my father.

****

"You niggas think it's sweet I see. Y'all not going to get away with snatchin me in my hood. I know y'all know who the fuck I be?"

"Yeah, we know who you going to be soon," one of the gunman said.

"Muthafucka, I'm Black Jesus, I run this shit!"

"Yeah, you use to run shit but that's over with. Matter fact just sit back and stop doing all that rapping."

The sprinter van pulled behind an abandoned house on the south side of Indianapolis. One of the gunmen slid the door open.

"Y'all ready?" he asked.

"Yeah, bring his bitch ass downstairs," a small man standing in the doorway demanded.

"Let's go bitch."

The two gunman that was in the van snatched Black Jesus up and escorted him into the abandoned house and down to the basement. It smelled bad down there. They were standing on top of trash, old musty clothes and even dead rats. The gunman escorted Black Jesus to a chair that sat in the middle of the floor.

"Tie his ass up," one man ordered them.

They immediately went to work wrapping the phone cords around Black Jesus' body.

"You marshmallow ass niggas think this is a game. When my people's find out I'm gone the whole mid-west going get shut down," Black Jesus said looking at all the mask men. "Show y'all face and look into my eyes. Y'all aren't no real killers," Black Jesus said smiling his million dollar smile.

"Who your peoples supposed to be?" asked one of the gunmen.

"Nigga y'all know I come from a whole bloodline of Jesus'. They call me, Black Jesus?"

"All okay that means Big Jesus supposed to come and help you? Y'all hear this bitch ass nigga. He think Big Jesus going to find us and kill us."

Everybody took their mask off one at a time laughing. Black Jesus' head started spinning when he saw who was standing before him. His entire body locked up as disbelief washed over him. One of the men was his dad, Big Jesus. The very same man that had him.

"Why Big Jesus?" asked Black Jesus.

"Why not son? I'm taking my seat back at the top where I'm supposed to be."

"So what happens next, Big Jesus?" refusing to call him Pops.

"For you to say I'm the best."

"I will never say no weak ass shit like that. You a snake and you can never be the best. I'm the G.O.A.T," Black Jesus said laughing.

"Oh, you think it's a game and you will say I'm the best. We going to start by slicing your body and pouring bleach all over you. Then we will go on to fingers and toes. Hand me that knife," Big Jesus said to his flunky who quickly ran to grab it up. "Now call me the best?" Big Jesus said while slicing him up all over the top half of his body.

"You a clown nigga," Black Jesus said gritting his teeth. "Ahh..." screamed Black Jesus. His skin was cut to the white meat and blood spurted down his body.

"Now let's do this again. Say it?"

"Clown ass nigga!" yelled Black Jesus, as he spit on Big Jesus chin.

"Pull his pants down," ordered Big Jesus.

"What you trying to do see how bigger my nuts are!" snapped Black Jesus,

"Nah I'm about to make you scream."

"Just do what the fuck you got to do because I will never call you the Goat," Black Jesus said.

Big Jesus because slicing at his dick and balls. Then he poured bleach all over him. Big Jesus had managed to turn a few of the workers in Black Jesus camp against him. He slapped Black Jesus so hard across the face it rocked the chair he was sitting in.

"Finish this work down here," Big Jesus ordered and he handed the knife to Dro.

Just like that Big Jesus was back at the top. He walked out the basement crowing himself the Goat. Dro and the rest of the gunman finished Black Jesus. They began cutting up his body. They were going to leave body parts all over the city and Black Jesus home.

Chapter 2

The next morning I walked to the station on 29th MLK to grab me some chips and something to drink on. Black Jesus didn't come home last night so it was hard for me to go to sleep. I cried most of the night. Since I could remember Black Jesus always made it home to tell me, he loved me. As I turned the corner back on 28th, I saw cars and people everywhere making it impossible for cars to continue down the block. I began to run up the block towards my house. Police cards and yellow tape from the crime unit had our house blocked off. I went to go under the tape when a lady told me to hold on.

"I live here. That's my house," I said pushing her hand off my chest and tried to move on, but she held her ground.

"Just hold tight and let me get the woman of the house, but you can't come in because this is a crime scene."

I saw another lady cop escorting my mother out of the house. My mother was hysterical. She was screaming, kicking and yelling at the top of her lungs.

"Momma!" I yelled to her. I took off full speed towards my mother who met me halfway. When I went into her arms I looked up at the house and saw an arm nailed to the house with blood dripping from it.

"Momma, are you okay?" I asked happy she was okay.

The same lady cop helped my momma to an awaiting squad car that was out front. I felt absolutely bad as I watched my momma breakdown. My whole life she been strong but that day she let it all out.

My momma as the most beautiful woman you'd ever met. I'm talking about inside and out. Momma was a petite brown skin with red dreads, who stayed laced in nothing but the best. She was in her mid 30's but acted like she was still 21. She would always tell people I was her little sister when we were out and that always made me laugh because people went for it. She even made me stop calling her momma saying it made her feel too old and to call her by her name, Kenya. She was one of my best friends. When I was about ten she would let me sip wine with her. She told me she would rather me drink with her than be out in the streets drinking where someone could put something into my drink. We just had that type of relationship. My momma was a solid chick too. We would spend nights where she would tell me stories about when her and my pops would be grinding or in the middle of a shootout and she would be right there with him.

As I stood there thinking about my momma, I looked up again and saw the arm. The same that belonged to my pops. It had the same shirt he wore last night.

This can't be real. My pops is Black Jesus, he wouldn't let anyone get him like this I thought. But there was no denying it, I couldn't hold down the chips and pop I had just ate and drank. I threw up as my knees buckled.

My auntie that was my age and Black Jesus little sister slipped past the tape and ran over to my side.

"Queen, get up," she said trying to get me to stand but I couldn't because I was throwing up my insides right there on the front yard. "Come on niece, I got you girl," Aunt Marilyn said.

Aunt Marilyn was my other best friend. We had been around each other since we were born. We were the same age. Our birthday was the same month. Everyone thought we were sisters because we had them eyes and same skin tone. Aunt Marilyn stood 5'2 and weighed about 130 pounds and a skin tone lighter. Where I stood 5'3 and weighed 145 pounds. We both had good long wavy hair, so we would celebrate our birthdays together the whole month. Everybody thought we were sisters.

I didn't understand how they could mail his body part to the house. This hood always be bumping with someone out getting money on the this block. But today the days nothing, no one out, I didn't add up to me. Our house was in the middle of the block. Every house on the block had someone from my Pops camp in it. Black Jesus had the whole block under security surveillance. Then you had my father dad who stayed at the beginning of the block so I didn't understand how anyone could have the balls to come on this block and disrespect Black Jesus. I heard my grandpops voice coming near the back of me.

"Let me get through this fucking tape, this is my son's house!" Big Jesus demanded pushing past the two officers that tried to hold him at bay.

"Daddy!" screamed Aunt Marilyn. "They killed BJ, daddy," Aunt Marilyn yelled to Big Jesus.

"I know Baby girl," Big Jesus said with tears rolling down his face. He kneeled down and hugged me tight. "I swear to you grandbaby, I'm going to find out who did this, that, I promise you. You know Grandpa will stand on his word right?" Big Jesus said crying.

"They killed my dad," I sobbed into his chest.

"It's gone be alright. Grandpa is going to handle everything. Come and let's go down to my house."

We walked down the block to Grandpa's house where everyone was gathered around standing. All I could think was how can these niggas was be standing here now but just 20 minutes ago no one.

"It's gone be alright Queen, baby. Auntie is gone help you out," Kym said while hugging me while we sat on the sofa. We all were seated in the front room looking at each other, nobody saying much with the exception of Big Jesus. He walked back and forth barking ordered into his cell phone.

11

"I want every nigga in the camp suited up asap!" He yelled, then threw the phone on the table. "Kym take Queen in the back and get her in the shower, feed her and lay her in the bed," Big Jesus said.

Big Jesus stood 6'2 and weighed every bit of 260 solid. He stayed in shape while in prison. He did 15 years but his swag was always on point. My dad and Aunt Marilyn was lucky to receive Big Jesus genes. I never got to meet my grandma but Aunt Marilyn and dad didn't take after him.

Big Jesus got his name from his father. That was they last name.

"Come on Queen, let me get you to the shower so I could clean you up," Kym said pulling me towards the bathroom.

I was in my own world at that moment. I really didn't give a shit about a shower but I still reluctantly followed her. Kym closed the door behind me, then started running the shower. She began removing my clothes. It will still around 12 o'clock in the afternoon.

Chapter 3

"No...No..."

"Queen, girl wake up," Aunt Marilyn shook me, waking me up.

I jumped up, tears rolling down my face.

"Calm down, Queen. You was having a dream. Daddy said he wanted to speak with you, he's outside waiting," Aunt Marilyn said.

"Okay, I will be out in a second," I said breathing hard. When I walked outside it was only five o'clock.

"Come on Baby girl!" Big Jesus yelled through the car window. I climbed in the passenger side of Big Jesus' Infinity QX50 which was all black on black.

"How ya doing?" Big Jesus asked. I just blew out some air while trying not to cry.

"I told you that Grandpa was going to find out who done this?"

My ears perked up as I looked over at him.

"Well I got him," Big Jesus said.

"Who was it?" I asked desperately.

"Let's take a ride," Big Jesus said pulling away from the curb.

Twenty minutes later, we were pulling in front of this house on Hardin and Edgemont St. A bunch of cars lined up the block. I almost recognized all of them. Dro's dark grey Cadillac XT4 was posted, then Hollywood black Escalade EXT was behind Crush black Camaro.

The front door to the house swung open as Big Jesus and I walked up. It was Dro standing with the door ajar.

"What's she doing here man?" Dro asked Big Jesus looking down at me.

"She's here for revenge!" Big Jesus said moving past him and down into the basement.

"What you doing standing there?" Dro asked. Without answering I began stepping towards the basement. When I got to the last stairs I saw my pops crew.

"Queen?" Hollywood said as if it were a question.

He was the youngest out of the crew. Now all eyes focused on me as I stood there. I was wondering the reason I was standing there.

"Come back here," Big Jesus ordered. I walked around the corner. I saw a man sitting in a chair tied up with a pillowcase around his head.

"Now this is why I called you down here because I told you, I would get the person who did this. Now isn't the time to cry but to get revenge," Big Jesus said snatching the pillowcase off the man's head.

I couldn't believe my eyes, it was my uncle Cash; the man who helped raise me. When my momma got home sick when Black Jesus moved here he sent for Cash to come and stay with us. He took care of me, Aunt Marilyn, the house and my friends. When my pops and momma went out of town it was him who feed me. "What is Cash doing tied up to this chair." I asked myself as my knees gave out.

"Cash!" I yelled with tears rolling down my face.

"Queen this is the man that took your Pops from us. The same man that ate your bread off the table." He hypnotize me as he continued to talk in my ear but in my heart I knew I shouldn't believe him. Cash wouldn't do anything to bring harm to the family. He wasn't in the streets and happened to have this own bag.

"Look at him the same man who your mom and dad welcomed into y'all house and loved him. But we got him now," Big Jesus said pulling a black and chrome .380 from his waist. He stood behind me and put the gun in my hand. With his hand still on mines, he raised the gun and pointed it at Cash.

Tears started rolling down my face again with fear.

"This is the nigga that killed your Pops, Queen so pull the trigger," Big Jesus whispered in my ear. Cash appeared to be coming to his senses after Dro slapped him. His mouth was taped but he began shaking his head as his eyes locked in on the gun.

"All you gotta do is squeeze, Queen and he's gone. Make your Pops happy."

"Boom!" The blast from the gun had my ear ringing. I didn't open my eyes to see if I had hit Cash, I just turned and ran up the steps.

"That's right Queen Bee!" Crush hollered out as I ran out of the house.

****

"Big Jesus, what are you thinking bringing that girl down here and have her do that. We all going to be locked up. You don't think she'll tell someone?" Dro asked.

"Yeah, for real Big Jesus, she's only sixteen." Hollywood said.

"Listen to you pussy ass niggas. Queen ain't gon say shit. Tell who? I had her kill Cash because with him out the way she would always look for me since I helped get her dad's killer. Cash wouldn't have never let Black Jesus murder go unsolved," Big Jesus said laughing while looking at Cash body. "Man, y'all clean up this shit. I 'ma go make sure my Grandbaby is doing ok."

****

15

"It's going to be okay, Queen, I did the exact same thing when I got my first kill back in '77," Black Jesus said. He was standing next to me while I threw up and cried. "Come on let's get out of here," he said as I stood up a little lightheaded but moved towards the truck.

All I did was stare ahead but kept seeing Big Jesus looking at me from my side eyes.

"Are you good Baby girl?" He asked.

"Yeah, I'm good," I lied.

"Listen Queen, your Pops would be proud of you. Today you showed heart you hear me? That slimy nigga, Cash, killed your Pops because he wanted his spot at the top. He's been stealing money from your Pops and he found out so Cash was trying to cover his tracks. I told Black Jesus not to trust him but he kept blowing my comments off like I wasn't talking about anything."

My mind went back to when my Pops would tell me that I would be the First Lady of Indianapolis, and all would bow to my feet.

"You hear me talking to your ass Queen?" Big Jesus asked.

"What do you want to eat? We were sitting at the through window of KFC on West 16th.

"Huh… Get me a famous chicken bowl and a water," I said snapping out of my trance.

"That's all you want? You got to start feeding your body, Queen." We rode around the city while Big Jesus told stories about when Black Jesus was a young boy growing up.

"I love you Grandbaby," Big Jesus said reaching over and pulling me close to him. He kissed my cheek.

Chapter 4

Today was Black Jesus funeral. By his request he wanted it to be held at Riverside Park, which is a park on the west side of Indianapolis that every goes to hang out at on Sundays to show off their cars. I have never seen the park so fat before in my life. People from all over the city and midwest had come to show their respect in the highest fashion. People were hopping out in suits, gators, jewelry, Jordan's, Airmax, Gucci, Prada and Polo. Most of the people I haven't never seen around until now, but I guess Black Jesus had done business with them at some point in the past.

Black Jesus expressed to my mom about having his funeral here a long time ago. I remember overhearing him say bury me on the same soil I'm from. The sun was out and not a cloud in sight. Last week of April use to be still cold but not this year.

My mom and I were seated in the front row right before Black Jesus pearl black casket with gold trim.

Big Jesus, Crush, Hollywood, Dro, Kym, Trina, Mercedes, Porsche, and Aunt Marilyn all sat right behind us. This was the only family Black Jesus had. He use to always tell me from time to time that family was everything but he also made it a point to let me know that just because a person share the same blood doesn't mean y'all family and that some times you had to build your own family.

I couldn't even look at the casket because every time I did I had flash backs of his arm nailed to the house. My momma had her arm wrapped around me as she prayed to herself.

Going back down memory lane thinking about the good times we had made my head hurt. It was always good times with him. He always put me and my mom first. We had family night every week where we all hung out and did whatever.

I had heard every story there was on how Black Jesus was a solid, stand up dude. People were sharing stories reflecting on how they knew him. A lot of people just got up there and made things up as they went on.

After everyone said their speech someone cut on the music and the real party started. My momma escorted me to the side so we could dance. We stepped to the music as she held on to her glass and a blunt.

"You're so beautiful Queen," she said smiling for the first time.

After about three hours of partying I was tired.

"You a'ight niece?" Aunt Marilyn asked walking up from behind.

People had started clearing out, so my momma was thanking everyone for coming.

"I'm ok," I said turning my face to her.

"Had to come check on you. You know I always got your back?"

"I know auntie," I said hugging her.

"So, when you gone come hang out wit the crew? We haven't seen or heard from you since all this happen girl. The crew is all in the house and they miss you so much. They wanted to give you space not trying to upset you," Aunt Marilyn said.

The crew was standing off to the side talking waiting to see if it was cool to come over. We were all family, but everyone knew Aunt Marilyn was my ace so they sent her over. When Aunt Marilyn gave them the okay head nod they all rushed over.

"What up girl," Mercedes said giving me a hug. Mercedes was the mixed one of the crew. Dad black and mom white. She was high yellow with green eyes and long hair.

Porsche was the tallest of the crew. She played basketball. She was brown skin with short hair that she kept done every week.

Trina was the one that always wanted to fight. Since everyone always told her, she looked like the rapper Trina she always screamed she was the baddest. Trina was brown skin also.

We all hung out with each other to the point people from other schools thought we all were sisters and cousins.

"Why you bitches over there acting all scared and shit. I ain't see none of you hoes get on any of these niggas," I said smiling letting them know everything was good.

"You know I got me a few numbers. I'm the baddest bitch," Trina said.

It felt good to be around my bitches. They were my family and I loved them as such. Whenever they were around which is most of the time and Black Jesus did for me, he made sure he did the same for them.

Chapter 5

The house wasn't the same without Black Jesus presence. He was the glue that kept this house and family together. He would get up early every morning and made us breakfast before I went to school and hit the streets. With him gone I still wanted to make sure Kenya had her breakfast on the table.

By the time Kenya walked in the kitchen I was setting the table for us.

"Good Morning Baby," she said smiling. "What are you up to this time of the morning?" She asked while cutting into her pancakes.

"Just wanted to cook you breakfast like Pops did! Would you like some juice?" I asked while pouring two cups. There was a knock at the door.

"I'll get it, sit back and finish your food," I said as I set the cups of juice on the table, then head for the door. "Who is it?"

"Papa, open up."

"Hi Papa?" I said opening the door.

"Just coming to check in on y'all. You a'ight?" he asked, stepping inside the house.

"Yeah, I'm okay."

"What's that smell, your mom cooking?" Big Jesus asked walking towards the kitchen.

I followed behind him, "Nah I cooked us a little breakfast. Take a seat and I will make you a plate."

"Kenya, how are you this morning?" Big Jesus asked with a smile as he leaned over to kiss her on the cheek.

"Could be better," Kenya answered.

When I turned around with Big Jesus plate I stopped because she was sitting in Black Jesus chair and holding Kenya's hand just the same way Black Jesus did. I felt disrespected.

"Queen, are you okay?" Kenya asked me seeing the color drain from my face.

Big Jesus turned to look at me to see what Kenya was talking about. I put on a fake smile and answered.

"I'm okay. Just started seeing back spots."

"Have you had any sleep yet?" asked Big Jesus.

"Probably not. When I woke up she was in here cooking us breakfast," Kenya said.

"I wanted you to ride with me, but I think you should get a few hours of sleep," Big Jesus said.

"Yeah Queen, go get some sleep before you pass out on your feet. I'll clean up the kitchen."

I wanted to get out that kitchen so bad anyway after seeing Big Jesus disrespecting my father and for Kenya not to see it pissed me off even more.

"Yeah, I think I 'ma go get some rest for a while. I'll see you later on Papa."

"A'ight Baby girl."

I left Kenya and Big Jesus to talk while headed to Black Jesus office.

****

"I have some shit to tell you about Black Jesus murder."

"Who did it," Kenya asked dropping her fork.

"Now I don't want you to get mad but I know it's going to hurt because it hurt me deep when I found out."

"Who the fuck it is?" demanded Kenya.

"Cash."

"Cash, my Cash?" Kenya asked in disbelief. She didn't buy it for a second, but in the back of her head she had been wondering where Cash had ran off too and "What happen to him?" asked Kenya.

"Let's just say he cooling with the fishes."

Kenya just shook her head. Black Jesus had coached her to never question him about what he did in the streets so she sat back in the chair. Something just wasn't right about it all. Cash was family and had no reason to kill Black Jesus or have someone do it.

"What you thinking about?" Big Jesus asked.

"This is just too much for me."

"I know Kenya and I'm here for you. If there's anything I can do, I mean anything, don't you hesitate to ask."

"Okay."

"How are you on money?" asked Big Jesus. He was trying to see if she had any Black Jesus big cash.

"I'm alright for now, but don't know for how long. Black Jesus safe only had about twenty thousand in it. It's more money around here somewhere, I just have to find it. Do you have any clue where he might've put it up at?"

"You know like I do he could have put that money up anywhere in Indianapolis. I know he didn't see this type of thing happening which was probably why it was only a few thousand in the safe. I know for a fact Black Jesus was holding a lump sum," Big Jesus assured.

He was happy on the inside that Kenya hadn't came across the money yet.

Kenya was eye candy and Big Jesus always had a thing for her ever since his son introduced them back in the day. At the time Black Jesus was coming up in the game.

"I 'ma tear this house up and see if I found anything," Kenya said.

****

I woke up a few hours later to the sound of Megan the Stallion blasting outside in someone's car. I peeked out the window to see all my girls and a few hood dudes. This one nigga, Money, was out there among the ground. He was the sexiest dude I had ever laid eyes on and if he'd just give a bitch the time of day he'd be the sexiest nigga I ever laid hands on. But he wasn't feeling me like that, I guess I was too young for him. He was always riding with this chick Oak. Oak was a little older and got money.

"Kenya, what are you doing down here?" I asked momma. She was downstairs going through bags, boxes and the sofas. She had all type of stuff on the floor.

"I'm trying to see if your daddy put any of his money in this shit. Do you know where it is?" She stopped to ask.

"What money?"

Kenya had hoped I knew something. I didn't know where Black Jesus put his money. He always gave me, his one and fives when he came in at night.

"Don't trip, Baby," Kenya said.

By the look in here eyes I sensed something was wrong but she didn't want to stress me.

"Are you good?" I asked sincerely.

"Yeah, it's good," she said flashing me that smile she was so famous for.

"A'ight well I 'ma 'bout to step outside. I just wanted to let you know. Do you need anything?"

"Nah, just be careful out there."

"Okay," I said going to hug her tight.

By the time I stepped out of the house, Money had disappeared. I scanned the group of niggas but there was no sign of Money.

"Who you scanning for? Money?" teased Aunt Marilyn. She knew me like I knew her and she knew how much I wanted Money.

"Nah, bitch, I was looking for your man."

"Bitch stop lying, you know yo' ass was looking for Money."

"If you hurry up you can catch Oak's car bending the corner," said Aunt Marilyn.

I hated the sounds of that bitch Oak's name. It tasted sour on my tongue. The only reason I didn't like her was just because she had her nails cuffed into Money. She wasn't no real threat. He worked for my dad. They called him Money cause he always had some type of way to get some money.

"Anyway, what's up girl?" I asked changing the subject.

"Ain't shit."

"Why everybody on the block like this? It's fat as hell out here."

"Yeah dad called everyone out," Aunt Marilyn said.

"All okay."

Everybody on the block moved towards where Big Jesus stood on his front porch. He had Dro on one side and Nate on the other while Hollywood stood in the back.

"I have called everyone out today to speak with y'all. Somehow or someway all of you are part of the team. We all know Black Jesus is gone and would be forever missed but the show must go on without him. With that said I'm the new Boss. From now on, you are to address me as Thee Jesus."

"We will…."Big Jesus speech was interrupted by dozens of conversations, whispers and outburst.

"What you mean call you Thee Jesus? Black Jesus was Thee Jesus of all the Jesus."

Pure was one of Black Jesus' friends and loyalists. He was the Chief of Security of all Black Jesus' blocks for the past few years. Since Black Jesus murder he had killed a few people on the team looking for answers. Pure outburst sparked several others to challenge Big Jesus' self appointed as Thee Jesus.

"Who crown their selves? The streets gotta put that crown on your head like it did Black Jesus. I wish I would call you

Thee Jesus!" Pure mocked. He turned and left and many people followed behind him.

Big Jesus was so heated from the disrespect. Niggas and bitches was waving their hands at him as to say fuck him. He cut his speech short. As soon as they stepped foot back inside his house he laid the law down.

"Y'all know what have to happen to those out there with the disrespect, so let's get it done!" he ordered.

Chapter 6

My mind kept wondering back to Big Jesus' little talk. Even though he was my grandpa the nigga was crazy thinking people was going to call him Thee Jesus. It only been two in a half weeks since my Pops been killed and he was already trying to step into his shoes.

While Black Jesus was stepping his game up and before taking the seat the war between hoods was at an all time high. But then Black Jesus took the seat and when it was beef OGs called on Black Jesus to be the middle man. Everyone respected Black Jesus because he was about his money, kept his word and wanted to see any or everyone eat. Big Jesus hated that his son did things in the streets he couldn't when he was running the streets.

It was 8:30 a.m. and I was up again making breakfast when out the blue the doorbell rung. It was Aunt Marilyn and Mercedes.

"What up bitches? What the hell y'all doing up so early?" I asked.

"We knew you would be up so we came to check on ya. What's that cooking?" asked Aunt Marilyn.

"Yeah, that shit smell good as hell," Mercedes said rubbing her stomach.

Aunt Marilyn rushed past me with Mercedes on her heels heading straight into the kitchen. We all were family so they knew they could eat.

"Hey sister Kenya, how're ya this morning?" Aunt Marilyn asked moms as she washed her hands, then a plate. Mercedes did the same.

"Hey sister Marilyn, Hey daughter Mercedes," moms said drinking some orange juice and turning to leave back out.

"Where you going Momma? You ain't gotta leave cause of these two bitches," I said smiling.

"Yeah sis, we just two hungry ass bitches trying to fill up their stomachs," laughed Aunt Marilyn as she buried her face back in her plate.

"Nah, they okay. I have to go make a few runs. But thanks for cooking," Moms said giving me a hug before excusing herself.

"So what up bitches? Y'all hoes ain't never up this early, especially yo ass Mercedes."

"This hoe woke me up," mumbled Mercedes.

"I wanted to let y'all know that me and Big Jesus talked last night and he said it's coo that we trying to get our own money but we have to only deal with him so we don't get played," Aunt Marilyn said in between bites.

"WHAT," I said.

"He said since Black Jesus is gone he can't stop us from pushing weed. We can't let your mom either so we have to watch each other's back."

"Is he still tripping like he was with that little speech?"

"Nah," Aunt Marilyn said.

With every word Aunt Marilyn spoke she had me, we always talked about us doing our thing better then the niggas because there wasn't a female crew out doing it big for the bitches. Black Jesus didn't want us to do anything. He always said it was the reason why he was out there. But now Big Jesus was on some other shit and I wanted to get down. I didn't care what the rest did but I would never call him Thee Jesus.

"So what's up bitch you in?" asked Marilyn.

"We like some fat bitches because we about to blow up," I said smiling.

"That's what I'm talking about. I knew you wouldn't let yo' bitches down," Aunt Marilyn said smiling.

"What y'all so hyped up about?" Kenya asked stepping into the kitchen dressed,

"Ain't nothing," I said.

"Hmm…Okay. Well don't let nothing get y'all into some shit. I gotta go Queen. If you need anything hit my line or text me," Kenya said.

"Where you going with that?" I asked noting that she was carrying Black Jesus black and gold box he kept his twin .45 cals in.

"Stay in a kids place," she said.

At that moment I knew she was up to no good but I let it go.

"Yup, see you later," I said.

Soon as the front door shut, Aunt Marilyn picked up her phone.

"Time to call some dick and see what they day bring us," she said.

"Hit Duke up," I said.

"You just want to see Money," Aunt Marilyn joked before talking into the phone.

Duke was Money's little cousin and they were always together, so if Duke came through, nine times out of ten Money would be among the group too.

"They on their way," Aunt Marilyn said getting off the phone.

"Who?" I asked.

"Duke and his crew," Aunt Marilyn said.

"Damn it's almost 10 o'clock already. We been sitting here talking for hour in half. Shit about to change for us now we can get money," I said clicking my glasses with theirs. "Let me go get ready."

I rushed off towards my room. I had to look cute if Money was gonna be in the house. I rum through my walk in closet looking for a cute outfit and end up grabbin this brand new green Prada shirt with a white Prada skirt to match and some Prada heels I got months ago.

I stepped in front of the mirror in the hallway to check my swag one more time. Satisfied that I was on point. We had a pool in the backyard and that's where we always chilled at. Nobody was allowed inside unless you were family.

"Look at Queen bad ass," Aunt Marilyn said to Mercedes as I stepped out the back door.

Niggas and bitches were everywhere. All we ever had to do is call one person and the hood came out. It was warm outside and nothing else to do but have fun. Duke and his click was on deck. All of 'em were wearing swimming shorts with their shirts off chilling by the pool.

"Queen!" Aunt Marilyn yelled, waving me over. She and Mercedes were setting the drinks and food out that we were goin to cook on the grill. We had hot dogs, burgers, beers, hard drinks and weed out there.

"What up?" I asked joining them at the table, but still scanning the backyard in search of Money.

"Where the ice at?" Aunt Marilyn asked.

"Go look in the deep freezer like you don't know," I answered.

"Don't worry niece, he's here. He just stepped out for a minute. Matter of fact, there your boo go right there," Aunt Marilyn said nodding in Money's direction.

"Damn...," I said taking in how fine he was. He had his shirt off showing all his tattoos and six pack. I stood there watching his every step as he joined his click. It was just something about him that had me hooked. Whenever we were around each other my heart sped up and my hands gets sweaty. And when he looks at me... Kind of how he's staring in my eyes now.

"Why don't you make some drinks, while me and Mercedes work the grill," I said to Aunt Marilyn.

"Bitch you can't hold back forever. If you want the nigga you gonna have to step up and stop been a little punk. I never seen you back down to something but talking to that nigga. Just pull up on him and tell him y'all going to dinner on you because I know for a fact none of them hoes paying for shit?" Aunt Marilyn said standing next to me.

I blocked out all that was said and decided to holla at a few niggas just to see if Money would notice. And sure enough he and Duke made their way over to where I stood and interrupt a conversation I was having with Eyes and Ton, two little niggas that had a reputation for tricking all their money.

"What's up…Excuse us," Duke said throwing his weight around. He knew the two niggas didn't want any smoke with him so they just walked off.

"Why you come over here hating and shit Duke?" I asked.

"I know you can do better then them," Duke yelled so both of the little niggas could hear him.

"I was just passing time."

"Yeah. Anyway let me get something to drink."

"Nigga get your own drink I'm not your lady," I said pouring myself a glass of wine that I got out of Kenya's wine room. That wine was for me only.

Chapter 7

The next day me and the girls all met up at Aunt Marilyn's house so we could talk to Big Jesus about letting us get some money. To our surprise we weren't the only people there when we pulled up. It was a few cars out there. When we walked inside the house it was a few faces from the hood and some from Hard Part. We didn't have any beef with them but we just didn't fuck with them most of the time and it was the same way with them.

Big Jesus knew that the old heads wasn't going for the law he was putting down but understood to keep his feet wet he had to deal with the young people because they were his future and they were the only ones that would follow him.

"I want everyone to listen and listen good. I hand picked you all because I see that y'all are hungry. Y'all are tired of the older group getting money while y'all stand on the sideline. This is what I'm going to do. I'm going to front y'all the work that way y'all can build y'all own money. Y'all get a cut and I get a cut so we all win. But if you take my dope, you pay for my dope if something happens. This is a grown ups game. Naw don't grab shit if you can't handle it. We have this and this," Big Jesus said holding up a large bag of dope and weed.

What Big Jesus explained was you could make more money off the dope than the weed. Some of them Hard Part's took both just like we did. Our ground work was already put in place since Black Jesus had the spots jumping anyway. He also informed us that there would be no exception to the rule because snitching was forbidden in the streets. He continued to schooling us on the game which I already knew since Black Jesus been doing that for years. Big Jesus also said he was shutting all the spots down and taking it back to the 2000s where people stood on the block.

After the schooling on the game we all bounced towards the door ready to get money but before Hollywood handed out cellphones that was only to be used for them, whatever sack you wanted and a gun. The girls got a .25 Cal and all the dudes got .9mm.

Aunt Marilyn and I appointed ourselves the leader of our crew. Big Jesus knew by doing what he was doing in no time all the young people would be under his wing. My only concern was getting money out on the block was one we all were girls and two Kenya seeing us out there moving. It wouldn't be new for us to be out there but anyone with eyes would see the dope fiends coming to us. Kenya had always treated us girls as adults and let us make out own decisions but we wasn't sure how she would act towards us hustling, especially standing on the block.

Being the baddest bitches that we were, we passed off the drop to Trina's brother for $1,500. Aunt Marilyn and I told the crew it would be better and safe to do it like this. We give Big Jesus $500 and we split the $1,000 then do all over again. But the second go around Aunt Marilyn and Porsche wanted to be out on the block so we busted down half the sack and I saw how they were out there calling shots like a vet.

After about a week we had 28th doing numbers. We were making about $5,000 a day, Monday through Sunday. Every night after we were done grinding we all go to my house, smoke some weed, count up our bread and take Big Jesus cut out for the morning. In exchange he would hand me a sack which I would bust down for the crew. Money was coming so fast and so much of it that all I could do was hide it in my room. I was still spending money Black Jesus use to give me.

For the past few weeks I kept up with cooking and cleaning the house. One morning while in the kitchen Kenya throw me a loop when she came in and said, "Y'all girls make sure y'all be careful out there on that block." The comment took me a minute to process.

"What, you didn't think I knew what y'all girls been up to?" she asked.

My eyes popped out of my head from foresee of what was coming. I didn't want to lie and deny what we were out there doing but I did want to see how much Kenya knew before showing my hand.

"You don't think I know y'all been out there calling shots. I even know about y'all selling Trina's brother dope every time y'all get on. Don't you know about now that you can't get anything over my head. Remember this was my hood before yours?" Kenya asked.

I looked at her to see if she was pissed off, but she kept her poker face on so I couldn't tell. Her and Black Jesus always kept their cool so it was always hard to read their faces.

"So you want us to stop?" I asked coming right out.

"I never said that, what I said was y'all be careful out there. Your father schooled you since you were old enough to talk. You're all I have left and my only child. I'm not trying to lose you no time soon. Do you hear me Queen?"

"Yes," I answered. I was happier than a gay man with a bag of dicks.

****

The next morning I was the first one on the block. It was 8:16 a.m. when I walked out the house. The birds was out chirping. I wanted to be out and get some of that early money. By 8:25 a.m., the fiends were out. I directed traffic like the boss standing off to the side serving and sending them on their way.

"Cop and go. Got that Jesus. Cop and go," I said calling the dope by the name I gave it as I handled the traffic. I only had about a gram left of the sack and only been out for no longer than half hour when this white lady walked up on me.

"You working," she asked.

My mind flashed back to one day when Black Jesus and I was having a talk. He told me never serve anyone that's white in the hood unless you knew them before.

The woman tried to hand me a fifty dollar bill, but I stepped back and just looked at it.

"What's that for?" I asked.

"Come on, are you going to serve me so I could be gone?" the female asked.

My gut was telling me to cut out but my mind was telling me to serve her the last dope I had. I took the money then handed her the dope. Soon as the dope hit her hand cars pulled up and police jumped out with their guns pointed at my head.

"Next time don't serve a police officer," the white woman said shaking me down and found $2,620. I was glad that I didn't have more dope and that I had my gun stashed in the bushes. By this time everyone was now hitting the block and witnessing me get hauled off in the back of a police cruiser. Aunt Marilyn and my crew stood off to the side.

Aunt Marilyn gave me a head nod to say, what the fuck? I could only put my head down.

Chapter 8

Black Jesus use to make me watch shows about people going to jail and told me only silly people went and the reason was because they didn't know how to count their steps. I felt dumb sitting inside the Marion County Juvenile Center waiting to be process. I was sitting inside the bullpen that smelled like piss and shit. The tank was full of girls. I tried to appear normal and chill so I found an empty spot on the bench by the door. I sat there listening to the girls take turn talking about their boyfriends, other females and who was getting money. Most of the girls was going home and some was going to the back to wait for court the next morning.

After hours of sitting, my name was called by the deputy. I had given the deputy a name Kenya made remember just in case of something like this ever happens. The deputy, who was a thick black lady, escorted me to the room where they fingerprinted you. I was then escorted back to the bullpen to wait. By now the bullpen only had a few girls in it, and not one was talking like before.

"Hey girl, what are we waiting for?" I asked.

"We going to the back," she answered then started crying her eyes out.

"Yeah, this is the group that's not going home," another girl added as if she'd been here many times.

"This can't be the case. This has to be a mistake," I thought to myself.

"Come on ladies, we going to the back. Line up on the wall so y'all can grab y'all clothes and mat," the deputy said counting our heads as we walked pass.

They escorted us to the D-Davis an unit for the girls. When we walked in girls lined the walls, some played cards and one was on the phone. I got the cell number went to the room and laid down until I cried myself to sleep. I was awakened to someone knocking on the door.

"Breakfast girl, we have to line up," the girl said,

I raced out the room to go get in line for breakfast. My stomach was touching the floor.

When we stepped back into the unit my name was being called for court. Once we got to the top floor where court was held my name was been called again.

"Megan James."

"I'm here," I said.

When I walked inside the courtroom, I saw Kenya sitting there waiting on me.

"All rise court is now in session. The Honorable Judge Rock. Court is hearing number # 112201. State vs. James," the clerk of court advised on record.

"You all may be seated," Judge Rock said. He was a young black man who appeared to be no older than 35. He took his time looking over the case on his desk.

"Okay, I have read over this case. Is counsel present?" He asked.

"Yes, your Honor. Ms. Sport is here on behalf of the defendant," the lawyer said.

My lawyer stood. Kenya had retained her to represent me. She was also the lawyer of Black Jesus' cousin.

"And how would your client like to plead today, let's see the counts....Count one for drug possession/distribution," the Judge read off.

"Not guilty at the time."

"Okay, I am releasing the defendant until next court date in two months," the Judge said hitting his gavel.

I was escorted back to the same bullpen I was in when I came in. After ten minutes the deputy opened the door and lead me to another door that had to get buzzed. Kenya rushed over to me and hugged me tight then Aunt Marilyn.

As we rode back to the house the lines on Kenya face let me know I let her down. I had to start counting my steps before moving, I told myself, as I reached over and held Kenya's hand.

Chapter 9

Aunt Marilyn, Mercedes, Porsche, Trina and I posted up in front of my house just laughing about how scared I looked in the back seat of the cop car. I looked down the street and saw Big Jesus standing on the porch texting. When he was done his eyes zoomed in on me then a text came through my phone from him that said, "Queen! Get yo' ass down this block now."

"Man, I be back Big Jesus want me," I said.

Aunt Marilyn started laughing hard because she knew her daddy was about to rip me a new ass hole.

"Shut up bitch," I said as I reluctantly down the block.

Big Jesus slammed the door hard behind me that I almost jumped.

"Sit yo' hard head ass down," he ordered pointing to a chair.

I walked over to the chair next to Kym and took a seat. Kym cut her eyes at me and made a funny face, as to mock Big Jesus while he paced the floor and began his talk.

"What the hell were you doing out there serving white people?" He yelled.

I didn't answer him so he continue on with this speech.

"Your little ass think you grown. You out here trying to do too much. Everybody on this team has a role to play. And here it is you take it upon yourself to step into another role by been out there serving people without speaking to me first. You got caught with dope. How dumb is that? I expected more out of you, Queen. You going to give me what's owed to me but until then you work for free. I'm done talking to you," Big Jesus said as I was some bitch that he could just dismiss from his presence.

I felt real little at that moment by how he talked to me. I didn't like the feelings I was getting in my gut and it irked me… "But when you was acting like a peon what can you expect?" I thought as I headed back up the block toward my house.

"What happened? What he do?" Aunt Marilyn called out, but I blew past her and the girls. I knew what I had to do… "Oh you shitty you in trouble so now you mad at us?" Aunt Marilyn laughed.

I went straight to my hiding spot once inside the house. As I went inside my panties dresser I could tell someone been in my dresser because I had put them in a position only I knew. Sure enough, as I counted my cash I discovered that $2,600 was gone. I only had six grand left and I owed Big Jesus $1,500. I went to Kenya's room but she wasn't there. I then went to Black Jesus office and found her there rummaging through his stuff.

"What are you doing?" I asked, as Kenya put the box back where it was. She was sweating and looked really mad.

"Did you take some money from my stash?" I asked. I didn't really care I just wanted to make sure it was her.

"Yeah!"

"It's coo, but what's going on with you in here because you don't look too good," I said.

"Come here Queen," Kenya said as we stood in the middle of the floor. "I have something to tell you," she said looking down at her hands.

I knew something was up because Kenya only looked down when something bad has happened.

"Queen, your father left money and I been looking for it all over this house and can't find it. I need you to think of any place he might have put it," she said.

"I don't know, he never told me," I answered.

"Fuck!" She screamed.

"How much money do you now?" I asked.

"Baby girl, we're broke."

"Broke? How the hell we broke. I knew my daddy didn't leave us out like that, he loved us too much for that," I said. I counted two grand off my six, then handed it to Kenya. "Here!" I said.

"What's this for?" she asked looking at the money crazy.

"It's for the bills and food. All we have is a few thousand. Can you get me some dope from somewhere else but Big Jesus," I asked.

"Yes!" she answered getting up.

"Okay, hold on," I said rushing back into my room and going to my other hiding spot and counted out to two grand I just gave Kenya.

"Here's six grand and get me some dope," I said.

Kenya didn't say anything. She just put the money in her pocket and walked out the room.

I knew she knew a few people who would just give her the dope just be been Black Jesus wife. I also knew with Black Jesus gone dudes wouldn't fuck with me but try to fuck me. When I use to ride with him, he always showed me who was who.

****

After Kenya left I went back to Black Jesus ' office hit a button on his computer and the floor popped up under his desk. He had guns stashed inside. I grabbed a .380 with a pink handle and the letters QW engraved on both sides. That was the gun Pops got for me. The QW stood for "Queen's World." I tucked the gun, pulled one of Black Jesus shirts over the gun then hit the button to shit the floor back.

The only ones outside was Aunt Marilyn and Mercedes when I stepped back out the door. I crossed the street and walked down the block and knocked on Big Jesus' door.

Kym opened the door, moved to the side once she saw it was me. I walked over to the table where Big Jesus sat with Hollywood and Dro counting money.

"Here," I said tossing the money on the table.

"What's this?" Big Jesus asked picking up the money.

"Yo' money I owed you," I said standing there with my hands inside the hoodie.

"That's what the fuck I'm talking about. That's my bloodline," Big Jesus said with a smile pointing at me.

I looked at him in total disgust.

"When you owe, you always pay. How much is it?" He asked.

"It's a grand there?" I answered.

"So my guess is you ready to get back at it?"

"Without a doubt," I said heading towards the front door.

"Where you goin without the sack," Big Jesus said holding a zip lock in the air.

"Out of your house," I said.

"What the fuck she talking about out of my house?" Big Jesus asked Hollywood and Dro.

I stopped and turned back around to face him.

"Listen if you ever talk to me the way you did just morning it's going to be problems. My dad ain't even talk to me like that so I be damn if you do it. Also my dad raised a hustler so I'm done pushing your shit I'm no one's peon. I was the fool for even thinking you were looking out for us. I see you out for self. Your own daughter out on the pushing hard while you in this house hiding with your two man bitches," I said.

Kym smiled at me before I shut the door.

****

"Queen what's up niece. Why you actin' all funny? You okay?" asked Aunt Marilyn as I rushed back towards my house.

"Yeah, I'm okay," I said not stopping to talk more.

I sat on the window ledge waiting eagerly for Kenya to pull back up to the house. Every time I heard a car come down the block I looked out the curtains. She had been gone for almost three hours and it was starting to scare me. I heard the sound of Rihanna "Bitch better have my money" blasting. I raced to the front door and snatched it open.

"Did you get it?" I asked as soon as she stepped inside the house.

She walked into the kitchen where she pulled a Ziploc bag of gray looking powder out of her handbag. She sat the bag down on the table and said, "Don't put your hands on nothing. I'll be right back."

Kenya disappeared into the back, a few minutes later she returned carrying Black Jesus scale, large Pyrex glass pot, some foil and some white powder she said was called Fentanyl that Black Jesus used to cut his dope with.

"Pay attention. You need to wear gloves every time you do this and you can't use a lot of fentanyl because it will kill them. If you touch it you would be dead too. This will be the only time I will show you this," she said.

I was like a kid in the candy store. I paid extra close attention to her every move and asked questions along the way I needed to know. Kenya got the work from Black Jesus friend Mookie from the Chicago. He was the type of dude that wanted to see anybody come up in the game. He gave Kenya the playa's price on the heroin and fentanyl. He gave her 4 ½ ounces of raw and ounce of fentanyl. The thing was she wasn't going to use the fentanyl since the dope was raw. She also let me know heroin weigh different because their zips was only 25 grams. She put each ounce on the scale and they all came up to 25 grams.

"Listen since this dope is raw you can sell it to the hustlers for $120 and let them do whatever but if you going to bust them down for the fiends you sell half grams for $150. That's $3,000 off the hustlers a ounce and if you do the fiends you would pocket $3,750. The key to this game is get the dope gone fast so you can re back up. Remember Queen if you can control your emotions, and pussy you would be able to do what you want. A woman that shows how to think is a dangerous piece," Kenya said giving me some game. "One more thing keep this dope inside the foil and hide it in the freezer because that keeps it fresh."

"Okay, I can take it from here," I told Kenya grabbing the foil, scale and dope off the table and rushing to my room to bust them down.

Chapter 10

I had to moved one step at a time because I wasn't going to fuck up again and land back in jail. I had to come up with a plan to sell this dope and not be standing on the block. I paced my room thinking hard while constantly looking at the foil sitting on the table in my room.

"Quick flip. Get it gone!" I heard Black Jesus and Kenya's voice echoing in my head. "Bingo!" I thought racing to the table. Black Jesus never went hand to hand on the block. He was always flipping fast. It all made sense to me now, Black Jesus would sell to people at a good price and kept good dope. My plan was just as Kenya said give it to the hustlers for $120. I wasn't going to sell to the fiends just yet. Just as I finished thinking, the doorbell rung. It was Porsche. I scanned the block before opening the door wide to let her in.

"What up, girl?" I asked shutting the door.

"Nothing much, just coming to check on you. You been on some solo shit since you came home. What's up?" asked Porsche.

I knew I could trust Porsche because me and her were friends way before the other girls came around.

"Sit down, bitch. I was just about to fry up some burgers and roll up this blunt," I said. "I know you trying to eat and smoke."

"Hell yeah," Porsche said.

"Here," I said tossing her the blunts and weed. I dropped the burgers into the deep fryer, made some Kool-Aid while the burgers cooked. We talked about this and that while the burgers cooked and Porsche rolled up. I dumped the burgers onto the plates, then grabbed some slice cheese. I sat Porsche plate in front of her. She fired up the blunt as we both sat there eating. I bought up the conversation about us getting money.

"Girl, I told Big Jesus, I wasn't about to be on the block selling his dope anymore like I'm a peon while he and his two male bitches say in the house counting money all day," I said.

"What, you for real?" Porsche asked.

"Hell yeah! That nigga got his daughter and grandbaby standing on the block. What type of love is that. My dad raised me to be a leader not a follower. Shid you raised you too," I said.

"Yeah, Big Jesus do be tripping hard. Only reason I haven't disrespected him is because he's your grandpa and Marilyn's dad. So how you goin to eat now?" Porsche asked.

"I already figured that out. I'm not about to keep getting that nigga rich. Question is, what are you gonna do?" I asked tossing a gram on the table.

"What's this girl?" Porsche asked.

"I'm calling it Jesus love. It's a gram of raw for $120."

"For $120?" Porsche asked while eyeing the foil.

"Yeah, you can do you thing while you on the block with the girls."

"Look, you know Aunt Marilyn is our family, but we gotta keep this on the low cause her loyalty is with her daddy first. You feel me?"

"You don't think I know this girl," Porsche said.

"Well, look, I'm about to move around a little but we have to click back up later on," I said putting on my Jordan's.

"Okay I have to go get me some money anyway," Porsche said giving me a hug.

"Here," she said handing me six twenty dollar bills.

"This what I'm talking about!" I shouted after closing the door. Porsche was my girl so I knew she wouldn't go out and tell my business and she knew how to save money. I grabbed about fifteen grams put them in a little bag and hid them inside my pants. The police wasn't going to get any dope off me unless they pulled all my clothes off which I knew they couldn't. I put the rest of the dope up in a new spot where no one would find it and walked out the back door. I hit the alley because I didn't want anyone on the block to see me plus I was headed toward Edgemont.

"What's up Queen?" Sade asked recognizing me.

"Ain't nothing What's up with you girl?" I asked coming to a stop where Sade was posted in front of her house.

She had her crew out there getting money. You could tell she was the boss by how she was giving out dollars.

"What you came down this way to see how we out here grinding?" Sade asked.

I was standing there watching everything that was going on around me. "Nah, I actually came to holla at you girl on some business stuff," I said.

"What's on yo' mind girl?" She asked me.

"Let's take a walk to Kim's," I said leading the way. Once we were around the corner and out of anyone's hearing I began with my speech. She grabbed all fifteen and told me she would be at me asap. By the time we were walking back, we were done chopping it up.

"Remember, keep this shit on the low," I said after giving her my number.

I made it back around to 28th and saw Porsche and Trina out there serving. Aunt Marilyn wasn't no where on the block. It was a good thing because I wanted to get Trina on the team too.

"What up girls?" I asked approaching them. I need to holla at y'all," I said acting like I haven't talked to Porsche already.

"What's wrong girl?" asked Trina pulling her hair into a ponytail.

"Nothing like that girl," I said laughing.

"I got some dope for sale and it's for the low-low."

"What you talking about Queen?" asked Trina.

"I got them grams. You give me back twenty and I give you a gram of raw. I know y'all bitches tired of having the same dope as everyone else around here and plus y'all only getting Big Jesus and Aunt Marilyn rich."

"Bitch, you ain't never lied," Porsche said nodding her head.

"Come on, follow me," I said leading them to my house. I went to my spot pulled out a few grams and came back into the kitchen and toss them on the table. "Them grams are bigger and the work is better," I said watching them examine the dope in their hands.

"So, girl, you gone give us these for a buck twenty a piece?" asked Trina.

"Look all you got to do is bust it down with the dope all have just sell it and pocket your money. Make sure to keep track," I said.

"Okay let me get all these," Trina said grabbing the two out of Porsche's hand then handing me four hundred dollar bills and four twenties.

"Don't say shit to Aunt Marilyn about this," I said looking at them.

"We got you bitch," Trina said.

"A'ight, holla at me when y'all want more," I said letting them out the front door.

Chapter 11

Word had spread through the streets that I was the bitch to see that had that raw and selling fat grams for buck twenty. People was pulling up to the crib at all hours of the making it hot. I knew if the streets was talking then Big Jesus had heard the talk. I don't know who put the word out there. The past few weeks I had been grinding no stop. I had ran through the dope I had and was up to nine ounces. I had mastered the art of flipping fast.

There was so much traffic coming and going through the house that Kenya said something to me one day about it blowing up in my face.

"You don't hustle where you lay your head at. And remember yourself, your business is a brand; An image. When selling any product, you must project an image of success," she told me.

What I got out of what Kenya said was so my dirt elsewhere so home could always be safe and to hustle like I'm running a business. I have never seen Black Jesus do any business out of the house. Once he was in the house for the night it was over with. I didn't want to disrespect the house so I got the keys to Black Jesus old Camaro and paid Duke to drive me around to make my sales. He been having this same car since he was 19 and it still smelled good. Every morning Duke and I would go get breakfast then make our rounds dropping off work on people around the city.

Duke and I was grinding tough together. After we finish off our sack for the day we would ride around the city just smoking and doing us. Duke would be stunting on niggas testing them. Everybody knew Duke was about that drama and that was one of the reasons why I had him by my side. And the fact that Money was around was a plus too. People was buying grams left and right all day and I was establishing my name in the streets as "Queen of the City" and not Black Jesus daughter. When people saw that Camaro they already know it was bosses bending the corner. But trouble was always around the corner.

One day the girls and I were at Riverside Park, just chilling like everyone else listening to music. Niggas were playing ball, dice games going on, kids run around in the water having fun while the females did their best to get some niggas to see them. While we were listening to the music some 2G bitches came walking pass talking shit.

"Them bitches think they the shit," we heard one say to her friend.

"What was the slick shit?" Trina asked.

None of the females said anything.

"Scared ass bitches," Aunt Marilyn said lighting the blunt she had just finished rolling up.

"Ain't shit scared this way and if you see a bitch slap a bitch," one of the girls said walking back towards us.

Just like that the entire park turned into one big riot, LAND-LIFE vs. 2G as Aunt Marilyn slapped fire from the girl. I swung off on the one standing by me as the others got to getting on with my crew. We all was going at it until someone started shooting in the air.

It was time to go so everybody rushed towards the Camaro.

"Y'all see how hard I slapped that bitch?" Aunt Marilyn asked laughing from the back seat.

"Hell yeah," I said laughing hard. "But you should've seen Trina beating that poor girl ass. Her eye was shut," I said still laughing hard.

"I know one thing, that bitch made me drop that blunt of loud," Aunt Marilyn said from the backseat.

"Here, roll this up," Porsche passed Aunt Marilyn a fat bag of loud.

"Niece on another note you need to be careful out here with the way you been moving," Aunt Marilyn said out the blue.

"Girl what you talking about?" I asked.

"You gon' sit here and try to play me to the left like the streets not talking about "Queen of the City. The whole hood knows about you," she said.

"Yeah, so what?" I said looking her in the eyes.

"I'm just trying to let you know to watch out cause the streets been talking."

"What the streets been saying to point where you telling me to be careful," I asked.

"You know Big Jesus is still tripping. He told all his peoples not to come to your aid and since you wanted to be a big girl, they are free to do as if you were someone else," Aunt Marilyn said.

I pulled out my .380, held it up and said "I wish one of those niggas or bitches pull up on me with that weak ass shit that would be their last time trying to get at the Queen."

"Calm down, niece. I know you going to handle whatever comes your way. I'm just putting you up on game. I get you though niece," Aunt Marilyn said.

Chapter 12

"Since she want to be a big girl out here in these streets then I'm going to treat her like she isn't blood and show her it's not a game. I can't have her out here selling better work without any consequences. Soon every little Muthafucka is going to be like fuck me and getting the work from her," Big Jesus said while riding the hood clocking everybody to see if they were pushing their own dope.

"You see that shit," he said pointing to a long line of cars on Udell. "Ain't no way Muthafucka can try and tell me that business is slow."

"Yeah, what you want to do?" Dro asked from the passenger seat.

"Something I should've been done when we first heard about her selling her own dope."

****

Me and the girls smoked and sipped wine all night that I didn't remember passing out. I grabbed my phone off the table next to my bed and looking at the time, it was almost 12:30.

"Fuck," I cussed as I hopped up and rushed into the kitchen to begin breakfast. I wanted to make sure Kenya got her breakfast just as Black Jesus sis. I remember hearing Black Jesus tell someone from his crew that you know when someone had changed when they no longer keep up with their same routine. It could be for the bad or the good.

Walking through the house I could smell food in the air. When I turned the corner to walk into the kitchen Kenya was at the stove doing her thing making steak and potatoes.

"Hey mom," I said hugging her from behind.

"Good Morning baby girl. I see you woke that ass up. You out there doing a little too much?"

"Yeah I know," I said taking a seat at the table.

Kenya was setting the table when a breaking news flashed across the television in the kitchen.

"Mom turn that up," I said.

It was Duke's house. I could see most of the hood in the background as the cameraman zoomed in. An examiner pulled a stretcher out of the house with a body on it. The white sheet was turning red from the blood.

"Oh my God," Kenya said dropping the plate in her hand as a photo of Big Duke flashed across the screen. The anchor said that the victim, Duke Johnson, had been shot to death then set on fire. They called it a home invasion gone wrong and there weren't no witness. They said Lil Duke discovered his father body inside the tub when he came home from one of his friends house.

"Where you headed?" Kenya asked me as I hopped up.

"I gotta go check on Duke," I said rushing into my room to get myself together.

"You be careful out there," Kenya said giving me a hug and a kiss before I walked out the door.

"I will."

Duke stayed the next street over on 27th so I went through out backyard and came up through vacant house and walked down to where everyone was posted.

"What up?" I asked walking up.

"Bitch they killed Poppa Duke," Aunt Marilyn said as if she knew who did it already.

"Who are they?" I asked.

"Shit, we don't know," Aunt Marilyn said. "I know me and Duke was coming from the store on our way to grab some smoke when we turned the corner we saw two dudes running out of the house. We didn't think nothing of it until Duke went in and saw what they did to his dad," Aunt Marilyn said breaking down crying.

"So, you mean to tell me that nobody on this block knows anything or didn't see shit. All these nosy ass bitches on this block and not one of the seen anything?" I screamed loud.

"Queen, calm down. Come on let me get your ass back around the corner," Kym said escorting me towards her car. "What the hell wrong with you out there doing all that yelling like you have bumped your head or something," Kym said pulling off down the block.

"You know it's hard for me to believe that for the second time that someone get killed a block over from each other and not one of them nosy ass people seen anything when they always out there."

"Queen you know how the streets are. Even if you did see something, you don't talk about it. That's the way of the streets."

"Nah, you don't see where I'm coming from," I said.

"Well break it down to me."

"Look when my daddy was killed they had the balls to come on his block and dump his body parts on his house and nobody seen anything then. He was Jesus! Then someone comes and shoot Duke's father and burn him up but no one seen anything! Shit isn't adding up to me around this bitch," I said hitting the dashboard of her car.

Big Duke's murder did something to me. I knew how Duke felt because not too long ago I was standing in his shoes. I could tell by the way Kym's eye twitched that she wanted to say something.

"I know there is rules in the streets but I'm not talking about go to the police, I'm talking about keep it in the streets," I said.

"Queen, Big Jesus and his peoples got the one who did that to your dad. Cash killed him, am I right or wrong?" Kym asked.

"Girl, Boo. Uncle Cash didn't have shit to do with that, but in the end he took the blame for it. My dad showed me how to use my mind so I know how to play chess. Cash was a chess piece. I don't know who did it but I will find out one day," I said.

Kym's eyes popped out of her head as I finished making my statement.

"You know well as I do, Cash wasn't no killer," I said.

****

"That's what I'm talking about," Big Jesus said while watching Fox 59 news with Dro, Crush and Hollywood.

"Since these muthafuckas want to be grown out there doing their own thing we going to show them better than we can tell them. Y'all see any of them out their selling a piece of candy, y'all lay they ass down. Shit, we paid so we can sit back for a while so if we have to we will turn this whole hood to a war zone."

Chapter 13

Everybody was posted in front of my crib on West 28th smoking, drinking and paying our respects to the OG Duke. It was a little past 11 o'clock and niggas was still telling stories about the OG Duke. Somewhere in everybody's story OG Duke was giving game and letting them know what the deal was. Big Jesus even came to chill with us for a while.

"Boom! Boom! Boom! Boom! Boom! Boom! Boom! Boom!" We heard gunshots firing off. Everybody stopped and just looked around. The shots were so close it sounded like it was in our block.

"That sound like it was coming from Udell," Porsche said.

"Come on, let's go check on them since they were having their own farewell too for Big Duke," I said starting to walk over to the next block.

By the time we walked on Udell people were standing around. There was a crowd of people gathering in the middle of the block so we rushed to see who been shot.

"What happened over here?" Big Jesus asked moving the crowd out his way.

"We out here talking about OG Duke, and making sales when this truck pulled up. Doe Boy went over to the truck to see what was up when they started shooting hitting him all in the chest. I ran toward them busting back, but I don't think I hit any of them," Penny informed us. He was shaking like a snitch at a gangsta party.

"Doe Boy don't die like this," Big Jesus said as he kneeled over his body. "He don't look too good. Keep your eyes open helps on the way now," Bis Jesus said.

We heard the police sirens in the distance and that made us realize we were dirty out there on the block so we all walked back around to Big Jesus' house. We all sat there just looking at each other waiting on to see if Doe Boy made it or not. Doe Boy wasn't nothing but 16 years old but he was deep in the streets.

Big Jesus came walking through his front door about half hour later with blood all over his clothes.

"Is he ok daddy?" Aunt Marilyn asked.

"No baby girl. He died as soon as y'all started walking off."

We all sat there realizing that one day you here and the next you gone. Since Black Jesus been killed a lot of things have been happening that made my gut turn. How is people getting killed in the hood and no one seen anything. As I flipped my thoughts around in my head the front door opens up.

"The police found Pure body inside the dumpster in the old Double 8 Food parking lot," Crush said to Big Jesus.

"Hell nah. This shit getting out of hand," Aunt Marilyn said.

"Take me around there," Big Jesus said standing up. "I need y'all to stay here until I get back. Stop off the block," Big Jesus said as he left.

"Bitch this shit crazy as hell. Who y'all think doing all this killings?" Aunt Marilyn asked with a shaking hand.

"What you think it's the same person doing all this shit?" I asked.

"I hope it is. That way we only gotta deal with one person and not a lot," Aunt Marilyn said.

We all sat there for the next twenty minutes throwing different theories around but none of the stuff we were saying made any sense.

****

"All them girls are scared to death," Big Jesus said.

"Yeah, they had that look on their faces," Crush said as him and Big Jesus drove around the hood. They were the ones that put Pure body in the dumpster a few days back for the disrespect he showed Big Jesus when they had that meeting.

"See they in the house rethinking hitting the block now. All we have to do is this last thing, and shit would be back to normal," Big Jesus said.

****

Me and Aunt Marilyn stayed up all night talking. I walked to my house once Aunt Marilyn fell to sleep. As soon as I walked through the door Porsche text came through saying she wanted to grab some of that "Jesus." I knew she was trying to get a head start since the block was about to start jumping.

"What up bitch?" I said giving her a hug when I opened the door.

"Shit trying to get on so I can get out here and get some money," Porsche said as I handed her the dope.

"You trying to sip on a cooler wit me."

"Yeah."

"Somebody is around here bringing that murder game, and nobody has a clue of who or why," I said.

While Porsche and I sat chopping it up in front of the house, Oak pulled up in her brand new Charger and parked in front.

"Why the hell this bitch parking in front of my house," I asked Porsche. "She know we don't fuck with each other."

"She got yo man in the car with her," Porsche said seeing Money.

"Fuck both of they ass," I said mad.

Oak rolled the window down and said, "Let me holla at you little Queen."

"That bitch just stunted on you, bitch. She called you little Queen," Porsche said laughing hard.

"You think that shit is cute, huh?" I said looking at Porsche.

"I mean we can beat that bitch ass if you trying to. If you don't like the bitch, I don't like the bitch."

"Little Queen," Oak called again waving her hand through the sunroof.

"Let me go see what the fuck this bitch want," I said walking down the drive way. I walked up to the driver side window with my mug on my face, I asked "What?"

"Chill girl I just wanted to holla at you on some money shit. Ain't no need to be all hostile with me."

"Well get out and holla at me like a woman." I said stepping back.

Oak climbed out of the car, and we stood in the street, "So what? What business do we have to talk about?"

"I'm tryna to cop some good work and everybody keep saying you have it. At first I didn't believe it until Money told me that you were the one," she said.

"Well you got some bad information because I don't have anything. Everything I have I'm small dogging it out so I can get all mines."

"You know I know the game. My money is green and blue like everyone else so it's good."

"Nah, your money ain't good this way," I said starting to walk off back to the yard when she grabbed my arm tight.

"What you little ass think I'm posed to beg you to sale me some dope when I can just take your shit. I tried to be the bigger person but you got me fucked up."

I snatched my arm away and with my other hand I came slicing at her face and neck. She fell to the ground holding her neck while looking up at me.

"Bitch don't you ever put your hands on me or disrespect my name!" I screamed. My blood was pumping and I blacked out for a minute. My zone was broken when I heard Money yelling, asking me why I did that. When I turned I saw Porsche holding her 9mm heading towards Money.

"Porsche, no!" I shouted as she was standing behind Money ready to shoot.

"Money get up outta here," I said.

Money looked up at me and Porsche and saw that she was holding her gun at her side. He got up and took off down the block.

"I'm telling you bitch you should have let me lay his ass down next to his bitch," Porsche said.

"Queen! Get yo' ass in this fucking house and you too Porsche!" Kenya ordered.

Chapter 14

"Queen, what the hell were you thinking out there slicing that girl up like that? Then why you out there with a gun?" Kenya asked frightened as she paced in front of the door, while constantly peeking out the peephole.

"She put her hands on me and tried to take my stuff," I said sitting next to Porsche sitting at the table.

"And I was just making sure my sister was okay," Porsche answered.

"Do y'all understand what this mean?" Kenya asked but before I could say anything pounding started on the front door.

Kenya crept to the door and looked out the peephole. She quickly opened the door letting Big Jesus and Aunt Marilyn into the house. You could hear the police sirens.

"What the fuck has gotten into you girl? You're out here slicing people up? Don't you know that girl is out there in the street dead. And the police is on their way now. They want answers. What you going to do because someone going to say something?" Big Jesus said standing all up in my face.

"Didn't nobody say shit when someone came and hung my dad arm on this house or when someone shot Big Duke and lit him on fire but now they see shit," I said shaking my head.

"Nah. I told y'all ass this was grown ups business so you gone have to take this all by yourself, Baby girl," Big Jesus said walking towards the front door.

"Big Jesus please don't let them take my baby. You know she's all I have," Kenya begged him.

He knew he had Kenya at his fingertips now so he was going to help her, so in the end she will help him. Honestly he needed Queen to get out the way. That girl had cut into his profits. She had some good dope too.

"A'ight but for this to get done you have to go for my word. My word is the end," Big Jesus said staring into Kenya's eyes. "We got to duck Queen off somewhere until the streets stop talking. Let it get some murders in this city and this one will go to the end of their stack of papers. Do you know anyone out of town?"

"Yes she can go to Miami," Kenya said sobbing as she reached for her phone.

They stood right here before me planning on me leaving and not once did they ask for my input. I stood up out of my chair, looked at both of them and started laughing.

"I'm not leaving to nowhere," I said.

"Since Black Jesus passed, this girl been hardheaded. She haven't listened to anything I have said to her. She's getting out of hand," Big Jesus said.

"Queen sit your little ass down and shut the fuck up now. Hello," Kenya said into the phone.

"Ya ass gone be in jail with 65 years if you ass stay in this hood but since you want to be grown it's on you," Big Jesus said.

When he started talking that jail shit my chest got tight and I started gasping because I never wanted to go back there let alone 65 years. I was only 16 years old.

"Who gone sit on that stand and testify against me. They wouldn't stand a chance in the streets and have to move out of town?" I said to Big Jesus out the blue just to see what he had to say.

"It could be anyone of these muthafuckas around here. Maybe that little nigga Money, you did just murder his girlfriend that he loved," Big Jesus said.

"Money ain't gone snitch. He works for you so you just goin sit there and let him. Plus he know what the smoke is this way," I said.

"He might work with me but what does that mean when them police come around and start fucking up the way he's making his money. These his blocks too, he's from this same hood. My hands are tied right now as far as doing something to him. You can't bank on just because he's in the street he won't testify. What's real to you might not be real in his eyes. There's too much on the table to be risking right now," Big Jesus said.

"Soon as we can get you out of this house, you're gone. Go pack your shit," Kenya said.

"Before you go pack come over here and look out this window. You see all these people, police and news vans out there. This shit isn't a game. You better get your mind right. Just let the smoke clear and you will be good. Maybe a few months," Big Jesus said.

****

I felt like a little ass girl as I sat on the plane. I turned to look out the window and watched Kenya and Big Jesus stood there. Big Jesus had this big ass smile on his face while Kenya cried her eyes out. At that moment my heart turned cold. He knew he could have helped me out. I just didn't believe anyone would have snitched on me. I turned my head because I didn't want to wave back. This was my first time on a plane but it was coo. Out of all the things me, Kenya and Black Jesus have done we drove there. The last place Black Jesus took us was to New York where me, Aunt Marilyn and the girls shopped to max.

"Damn Pops I miss you so much," I whispered to myself before shutting my eyes for a little rest.

****

When the plane's tires hit the asphalt it made the plane shake causing me to wake up. We were in Miami, FL the Mia. The plane did a few spins around the tarmac before finally pulling in. Passengers began unloading the plane one by one. I grabbed up my few bags and fell in line behind this sexy brother.

The weather was hot as hell when I stepped out of the airport into the burning sun. I started sweating beans and I only been standing here for a few seconds.

I saw my name Queen on a board. This light skinned, cute chick with dreads wearing this business suit was holding the sign up in the air. She must have been Kenya's cousin Punkin. She told me to look for the dreads. I rushed over to her.

"You must be my little cousin Queen," the chick said with a pretty white smile as I approached her.

"Yes!"

"Well, I'm you cousin Punkin. It been a while since the last time I saw you. Come on, let me help you with those bags," Punkin said reaching down for one of my bags. We walked through the parking lot until we stopped at a white Bentley with pink insides. Punkin popped the truck and tossed my bags inside.

"I know you have rode inside of a Bentley before?" Punkin asked.

"Nah, my dad and moms only had Mercedes-Benz," I said.

"So Queen, you going to be staying a while with me and my daughter, Pooder. We have a little crib in Bel-Air. Any who, what did you like to do back home?"

"I just hung out, chilled with my crew and got some money," I answered.

"Got money, okay?" she smiled.

"What about school? And what grade are you in because school starts in a few weeks down here."

"I love school and I'm in the 12th grade."

I didn't know Punkin but knew of her and her husband Uno. They was getting so much money back a few years ago.

We pulled up to a crib that sat on the water. The mansion sat back with acres of private land. The land was so beautiful. My eyes popped out of my head as we rode up the driveway, which was laid out with two Ferraris, black and a gold one. Two Rolls Royce and a pink Porsche truck. The house was connected to a six car garage with a swimming pool in the back.

Punkin gave me a brief tour. When you stepped inside the house it was all black and gold. She had so much expensive art throughout the house, I didn't want to touch anything thinking I would break something. She took me up to the second level and showed me my room.

My room was cute, it has it's own bathroom, walk in closet, entertainment center and a big bed with pillows everywhere. The girls not going to believe this when I call them. It was far away from standing on 28th.

"Go ahead and get yourself together. I'll be in the kitchen if you need me for anything. Pooder will be here soon. And call your mom so she would know you made it," Punkin said before stepping out the room.

I laid back onto the bed pulled my phone out. I had to call Aunt Marilyn's phone first to see what was going on in the streets.

"Hello," Kym said picking up Aunt Marilyn's phone.

"Where my auntie at?" I asked.

"Queen? Where you been at?" asked Kym.

"I'm around," I said.

"Girl, boo. Anyway, are you okay?"

"Yeah I'm good. But where's my aunt at?"

"Oh you don't want to holla at me, huh?" Kym said.

"Girl that's not the case, I'm just tryna holla at my aunt about something important real fast," I said not trying to hurt her feelings because I didn't want to talk to her.

"Hold up for a second, she stepped outside I'm going to grab her for you."

"What up my bitch?" Aunt Marilyn yelled into the phone. Hearing her voice made me smile and light up.

"Bitch nothing. What's the streets talking about?" I asked.

"Your name is on everybody's tongue."

"I know the police been around?" I said.

"Hell yeah they been to the house like ten times already. They had posted a picture of you throughout the hood but people keep tearing the down. Bitches is out here saying you sliced that bitch up like she was some bread."

My mind went back to when I was slicing Oak up as I listened to Aunt Marilyn talk.

"You listening to me Queen?" Aunt Marilyn asked.

"Yeah, I'm listening to you just wondering how the police knew it was me," I said.

"You know how people are girl?"

"Have you seen that nigga, Money around?" I asked.

"Me and Porsche caught him coming out of Barbecue Haven and she pulled the heat on him. He ain't on shit," she said.

"That's good. Thank y'all auntie," I said feeling a little better knowing that I had some real girls in my corner.

"So how long you have to stay gone?" asked Aunt Marilyn.

"Bitch if it was up to Kenya and Big Jesus, I might be here for a few months. You see I didn't want to go in the first place."

"Just chill out and let shit coo off and you know we will be here with open arms waiting on you," she said.

"So what you into?" I asked.

"Same shit, out here chilling with the girls. Bitches say hello to Queen," Aunt Marilyn said turning the phone on speaker.

"Hey best friend?" Porsche said snatching the phone.

"Hey bitch. What's up?"

"Ah out here chilling wit the crew and a few niggas. Hold on."

"Bitch where you at? They said you were out here wiling the fuck out. Why you have to leave? Trina asked firing question after question.

"I will be back home sooner than later. I just wanted to say hello hoe."

I finished talking to the girls, then called Kenya's phone to let her know I was good. I tried her phone at least ten times but it kept going to the voicemail after the second which never happens. I began to unpack my bags, then hopped in the shower. The bathroom was the same size as my room back home. After taking a shower I tried to hit Kenya again but this time on FaceTime with no luck. I laid back and shut my eyes.

Chapter 15

Months later….

I had really gotten to know Cousin Punkin and Cousin Pooder, as I as called them now. Cousin Punkin knew a lot of things about a lot of stuff. I even learned a lot from Cousin Pooder even though she was only a few years older than me.

Cousin Punkin told me stories that I remembered from my dad. When I asked her things she always answered them. She never sugar coated anything with me.

Cousin Pooder was showing me how to do hair and nails. For her to be so young, she had her stuff together. For the first time I realized that it was more to the world than just sitting on the block hustling. They both came from the same soil I came from and to see how they were moving opened my eyes.

Cousin Punkin took me to her place of business called Diamonds 4 Everybody, where they specialized in diamonds, among other things. You could tell everyone loved her because the minute she walked inside that business all you heard was her name. She had a personal assistant that was so fine named Nelly who greeted her at the door with the stocks and some hot green tea.

"How are you today?" He asked her leading us into her plush office, and pulling out her leather chair for her to sit.

"Why is this angel so far from heaven and hanging with you?" He asked Cousin Punkin but smiling my way.

"I'm no angel, I'm more like the devil but my name is Queen and she's my Cousin Punkin," I said.

"Well coo then, Punkin if you need me, you know where to find me," Nelly said excusing himself but Punkin stopped him before he was able to shut her office door.

"Yes," he said in a sexy accent.

"After lunch I need you to take Queen shopping and help her get right for school. Pooder was going to do it but she has to work."

"Not a problem," Nelly said winking at me before shutting the door.

Knowing school was around the corner it had me home sick. It was coo chilling in Miami with my cousins that was rich but all my mind did was think about Indianapolis. I chilled around the business following behind Cousin Punkin learning new things until it was time for Nelly to take me shopping.

Punkin tossed her black Visa on her desk. She was on the phone talking business about some diamonds so we just headed out.

Nelly was laid back. As soon as we hopped in his Audi that hood swag kicked in.

"Damn I'm glad to be outta there," he said putting on his Snapback hat.

He was so fine from head to toe. He stood about 6'0 and was all muscle. He had a golden potato skin tone that made a bitch want to eat him. I thought Money was fine but Nelly took it a few steps up.

"So Queen where are you from? Nelly asked.

"I'm from Indianapolis. How about yourself?"

"I'm from Costa Rica."

"Why Miami then?" I asked.

Nelly laughed. "I'm down here because my people sent me a few years ago to stay with Punkin so I could get a better life. I started working at her business and going to school at night."

"What! You in college?"

"Finishing up my last year. I am going for business. I will have my own thing soon. I have saved a pretty penny working for Punkin."

"How old are you?" I asked.

"I'm 22. And yourself?" He asked.

"I'm 40 going on 17."

We continued to talk as we drove. I just kept thinking that a fine brother like himself has to have a woman. Then I wondered if Cousin Pooder ever did anything with him.

Nelly took me to a few boutiques. I wasn't feeling a lot of the stuff they had because most of it was for white kids. But I did go crazy shopping. I copped some clothes and heels from Caovilla, Chanel, Versace, Gucci, Prada, Fendi and Louis Vuitton then I went to grab me a few pairs of Jordan's, AirMaxes and Air Force Ones.

After we finished shopping it was about three o'clock so he took me to a place Cousin Punkin owned called Indy's Kitchen so we could pass time.

Chapter 16

Bel-Air High, the sign mounted over the school building read.

Cousin Punkin was taking me to enroll in school, today. I began the 12th grade. My last year in school. I missed my crew bad. We was supposed to be running Washington High School. I looked around the school and knew they haven't seen a girl like myself.

"Cousin Punkin, is this the only school I could go to?" I asked as we were walking through the main office doors.

She started laughing. "I'm afraid so little cousin. Them were the same words Pooder spoke to me when we came to enroll her," Cousin Pooder said.

"Hello Mrs. Punkin. May I help you?" A white women asked appearing from the back.

Cousin Punkin knew everyone in Miami it seemed like because everywhere we went someone was calling her name.

"My little cousin just moved with me and Pooder so I'm here to enroll her into school," Cousin Punkin said.

"Are you her legal guardian?" she asked.

"Yes, I have copies of the papers here."

"Okay, if you two will fill out these papers we will be done in no time."

I grabbed the forms from Cousin Punkin and filled them out myself. When I was done she signed them and went back to the front desk.

"Miss…" Cousin Punkin said waiting for the lady to come and grab the papers out of her hand.

The woman took a minute to look over the papers and said, "Okay, you may leave now. School lets out at 2:30pm."
I got my scheduled and headed to the first period, which was Geometry class. I walked through the door the first thing I saw was the name Mrs. Rush written on the board. Class was already started. All eyes shifted to me as my Louis Vuitton pumps echoed on the hardwood floor. Cousin Punkin stylish ironed my hair out so it had that fresh glow on it. I hand Mrs. Rush my schedule. She looked up at me with a smile then pointed to a seat near the middle of the class. I wasn't feeling this school at all because I stood out. The students as this school were a mixture of blacks, whites, Latinos and Asians. I walked to my seat next to this black girl who kept looking at me. She was a little thick with a chest full of tits.
"I'm Naomi," she finally whispered to me.
I just winked at her, but she kept on talking.
"Where you from?" she asked me.
"Be quiet back there Naomi," demanded Mrs. Rush.
Mrs. Rush was a young black woman who looked more like a nanny. When the bell rang, I looked at my schedule to see where my next class was and it was Language Arts.
"Let me check that out," Naomi said extending her hand for the schedule. "We almost have the same schedule. Come on, I'll show you where your next class is," she said.
"Who is your new friend?" a black chick asked Naomi as we were headed up the stairwell.
"I'm Queen."
The chick looked me up and down. "Betta let her know who runs this school," she said, then walked off.
"Don't sweat that bitch."
"Who is she?" I asked.
"She's in a gang called The Wild Girls and they always be on some bullshit starting trouble," she answered.
"They got the right bitch."

"Don't trip girl. Come on, let's get to class before we both be late."

The rest of the day kind of went fast. I was sitting in my last class. I kept looking at my Rolex watch Cousin Punkin let me have waiting for the hand to strike 2:30 and then the bell sounded off. I rushed out the door with books in my hand. Naomi stood by the door waiting for me to exit, we had said earlier that we would mob home together after school since she stayed down the street from Cousin Punkin house.

"You ready to go?" Naomi asked, as I came out the classroom.

"Yeah, let's get outta of here," I said following Naomi through the hall. As we were passing a group of dudes one winked at me and smiled.

"Who was that boy that just winked at me," I asked.

"The one with the waves name is Jay, then you have Mark with the dreads. They play for the school basketball team but the rest of them dudes are their peons," she said.

When we exited the school, I could see a large crowd standing outside the building. It was a group of females all wearing the same colors. I really didn't care so I kept it pushing minding my own business until the crowd of girls started walking toward us meeting us in the middle of the street.

"You on your own with this one Queen," Naomi said turning the other way.

I shook my head. The same female I saw on the stairs was leading the girls. I'm from Indianapolis so I knew what the deal was. I was new here so they were testing my gangsta. I was just glad I put my Jordan's on. I tried to keep walking like it wasn't nothing but the bitch grabbed my arm. While I turned to say something the rest of her crew formed a circle around me.

"Bitch, what hood you claiming?" asked the chick that grabbed my arm. She was a little thicker than me, but for the most part we stood the same height.

"I'm from Deland, Indianapolis fines," I said as I was digging for my knife or lock but before I could get ahold of either someone hit me in the back of the head. I came swinging the lock hitting one of them in the head drawing blood. I wasn't going to stand there and wait for help so I started swinging wild at whoever was by me. I heard someone screaming from their car so I swung again hitting the chick from the stairs in the nose and cut down the street. When I hit the corner I saw this chick laughing and waving for me to come, which she held her front door open.

"Girl if you don't hurry up you done!" she said pointing toward police cars zooming down the block. Not trying to get busted, I rushed over to her house. She shut the door as the police slowed down to see where I went.

"Girl good looking," I said holding my chest out of breath.

"No problem. I'm glad someone made that bitch famous."

Hearing the term famous was some Indianapolis stuff so the chick had to be from the city or know someone from there so I looked at her and smiled.

"What you know about making someone famous?" I asked.

"That's something we use to say back where I'm from. When someone get their ass kicked or killed that's what they say," she said.

"Where you from?" I quizzed.

"Born and raised in Indianapolis AKA Nap town for short."

"You're lying," I said.

"Seriously, look," she said showing me the Colts and Pacers symbol on her arms.

I still didn't want to believe her so I kept up with the questions that anybody from the city would be able to answer.

"What part of the city you from, cause I'm from there and them my streets," I said.

"I'm from Far East."

"Where at?"

"Post Road on 42nd Street."

"Okay one more question. We have two events that bring people from different cities. What are they?"

"Expo and Classic," she said.

"Damn girl what are you doing way out here in Bel-Air?" I asked.

"I had to beat this girl ass at Lawrence Central and they kicked me out and locked me up. My mom told the Judge either send me to girl school or here with my dad. How about you, what are you doing here?" she asked.

"Really damn near the same thing expected I sliced a bitch up bad?" I said.

"Well it's good to meet you. What you say your name was?" the chick asked extending her hand.

"Queen."

"Tiffany but everyone calls me Tiff."

"Alright girl. That's what's up then," I said.

"I think that heat is down now. If you want you can chill for a minute, and I can take you home," she said peeking out the front door.

"Yeah I will chill for a while. I appreciate the help."

"Well come on let me give you a tour of the house. It's not as big as the ones that sits by the water," she said.

Chapter 17

From the day we met me and Tiff hit it off. We would hang out every day like we been old friends. Cousin Pooder said she wasn't to be trusty because it was all in here eyes. I was just happy to be around someone from my city.

Tiff swag was on point. She had all the Jordan's and AirMaxes. The only thing I was up on is that I wore heels and business suits that I got from Cousin Pooder and Cousin Punkin. But she stood on her own and wasn't a punk.

Two weeks had passed since I busted that chick up. I was waiting for her and her crew to come back. A few days later she was back at school healed up with her sisters that used to go to the school. They had the school surrounded with their crew so they could get some get back on me. Tiff brushed my arm trying to get my attention to inform me that the bitches were outside waiting on me, but I was talking to this fine chocolate brother tryna get him to let me and Tiff throw a party at his house while his parents were gone to New York. Soon as we hit the exit doors all I saw bitches and niggas everywhere.

The next thing I knew was someone hit me connecting with my jaw. Those hoes wasn't playing today they came to bump. I shook the punch determined to stay on my feet, cause I knew if I hit that ground it was a done deal. I swung catching this fat girl in the mouth knocking her tooth out. I was wearing big rings and that was the cause of her teeth coming out. I felt a pain in the back of my head as someone hit me with a brick. But I kept throwing punch after punch.

Tiff stood with me. She had slapped the chick who stoled me with one of her schoolbooks. We end up with our backs to each other going at it punch for punch with them hoes until the sound of school security could be heard making the crowd disperse. I escaped that fight with a busted lip, knot on the back of my head. Tiff was bruised pretty bad taking that she was lighter. She took it like a bad bitch and for that she was my girl for life and gained my respect.

After that fight, we didn't have anymore problems with them because they knew we were down to getting it on any day of the week. They thought I was just some punk ass out of town chick until I showed them the truth. Our names were ringing in school that them Indianapolis chicks wasn't to be played with.

My birthday was coming up and I wanted to go home and spend it with my crew like we been doing for years. I been trying to holla at everybody but it seemed like they were out there doing them chasing that bag. I started to feel that they said fuck me and got a new girl to take my spot. I ain't even talked to Kenya since I been here. I felt like she might be taking this harder than me. I just didn't get her. I missed everything about the city and all in it.

Come to find out Tiff dad sold big dope across the map. She told me her dad was going to Cuba to pick up a shipment and he supposed to be going to Indianapolis to do a drop off to one of the big fish. She knew how much I missed the city and already asked her dad if we could ride with him to the city which was yes. Tiff was going to see her mom and brothers.

****

"Cousin Punkin, you know my birthday is coming up and I would like to go to the city to see my mom since I haven't talked to her. I really miss her, cousin so can I please go see her. Tiff dad is leaving to go to Indianapolis and said it was coo if you ok it," I said.

"I'm coo with you just make the trip for a few days," she said.

It was finally the day of the trip and we were to leave right after school. I skipped school so I could spend the day with Cousin Pooder. She gave me some money for the tip. We went to pick up from school and Cousin Pooder dropped us off at Tiff's where her dad was waiting for us. We drove straight to the airport. The jet her dad was suing to fly us back to Indianapolis smelled like it was brand new with that leather scent.

"Come here and check this out," Tiff said opening a cooler that were filled with ice and fish.

"Girl shut that shit," I said holding my nose.

"Nah, I'm trying to show you something," she said sticking her hand inside on the fish pulling out a brown wrapped object and tossed it to me.

"I read the letters "WSF." That was the same stamp Black Jesus was getting on his. I knew then it was a brick of raw heroine.

"Guess how much my dad get those for?" Tiff asked grabbing the brick back.

"How much?" I quizzed.

"My dad plug gave them to him for $10,000 in Cuba and over here they want between $65,000 to $90,000. My dad plug is from Indianapolis too," Tiff said.

"Damn $65,000 to $90,000!" I repeated.

"Shh, be quiet girl…" Tiff said, then put the brick back inside the fish like it was.

She never knew that I was just hugging the block with my girls nor did she know I knew what I could make off one key in the city. I had numbers jumping all around in my head that my hands started sweating. There had to be at least twenty ice coolers in the back and I knew each cooler had more than just one fish. When Tiff told me, her dad's name it didn't hit me until I saw his face that I seen him around my dad before. I sat back wondering how I could get on the level to where I can ship bricks across the map. I wanted to be that person one day.

After we stopped to gas up, we were finally flying over Indianapolis Airport waiting to land. I was so happy that I couldn't sit still. I watched as peoples and cars moved around. I had been gone for months now but it seemed like it had been years.

"Ah…Sweet home," I said stepping off the plane. While Tiff was busy getting their bags I dipped back onto the plane to the coolers where I took one of the fish out and grabbed a brick and put it in my bag. When I walked back off the plane Tiff and her dad were still loading the car with bags so I hauled ass through the airport to my waiting Uber driver. I paid him with Cashapp already so I rushed and hopped in the backseat.

"West 28th Martin Luther King, please," I said as I sat back. Yes, I did it! I was back in the city with a whole brick of raw.

Chapter 18

I told the uber driver to let me out right on the corner of 28th St. I walked up the block with my dark shades on and hat watching as the block jumped. I wanted to start screaming but kept my coo. I walked right up on everybody without them even seeing me.

"You bitches are slipping," I said taking off the shades and hat.

"Queen," Aunt Marilyn said rushing over to me. "Bitches, it's Queen! When you touch down? Kenya or dad ain't say shit about you coming back home."

"I know they didn't," I said happy to see my crew.

"It's about to be a party out here tonight bitch," Porsche said.

"Yeah, we about to do something nice for you," Trina said smiling.

"Mercedes, what's up bitch?"

"Shit hoe. I see you gotta dark," she said hugging me tight.

"So, how y'all been holding up?" I asked.

"We just been out here grinding trying to stay a step ahead of the police and these killers?" Porsche said.

"Yeah bitch, since you been gone away a lot of people been coming up dead. Ebony got killed at the club, Ke-Ke from Udell got killed at the light last week, Q-Ball got killed too. Everyday its something. Niggas been coming through shooting like crazy. We don't even grind out here at night anymore. We either chill over my crib or ride around doing us," Aunt Marilyn said.

I could tell everyone as scared as Aunt Marilyn gave me the run down on what been happening out in the streets.

"So what the police been on. Are they still riding around here?" I asked.

"Hell yeah. It's been too much going on around here and in the streets," Trina said.

"Here comes daddy," Aunt Marilyn said when she saw Big Jesus car turn down the block.

"Queen, get your ass in this car," he ordered as soon as he seen my face.

"I 'ma holla at y'all in a minute."

"What the fuck you doing back in the city?" Big Jesus asked as I shut the car door.

"That incident that happen been over with. It been months now," I said.

"Kenya never told me that she sent for you, so when did you get home?" he asked.

"Today. Look Grandpa, let me do me because I can stand on my own. Whatever come my way I can handle it."

"A'ight now, I want you to remember every word you are standing here saying," Big Jesus said.

"Let me take my own path. One thing I learned was every path you take leads up to a choice. Some choices change your whole life. My dad told me if I don't like something, I should change it and I'm standing her now telling you shit about to change," Queen said.

"Well okay then. You didn't like Miami?" Big Jesus asked.

"Yeah it was fun as hell just missed my city more," Queen said looking him in the eyes when she said her city.

"You just couldn't wait to get back to your dead ass city, huh? Well I'm not going to take up too much more of your time. I know your girls out there waiting for you."

"Yeah they are," Queen said opening the front door.

"Queen remember what you said?" Big Jesus said before she walked out the door.

"Where you headed to Queen?" asked Aunt Marilyn.

"I gotta put my bag up. I will be back in a hot second bitch," I said walking down the block towards my house.

****

"Kenya! Kenya!" I yelled as I walked through the house looking for her. The T.V. was on mute but had a porno on there with two wine glasses on the table. Kenya was in her room chilling, smiling from ear to ear as I stood in the hallway watching her rub up on some dudes chest as he laid back in her bed, the same bed my dad laid in. She looked up and saw me standing there. She wiped her eyes first like they were playing tricks on her.

"Queen," she said hopping up and rushing towards me like she was happy to see me.

"Who is that nigga," I asked not caring to hug her back. My eyes stayed glued on dude while he laid back in the bed sipping beer and smiling.

"Oh, that's Wes, a friend of mines," Kenya said looking everywhere but my eyes.

"What's he doing half naked chilling in my dad bed," I asked with an attitude.

"Excuse you, but I'm grown and this is my house the last time I checked," Kenya said loud.

"So this why I heard from you in months. Fuck me now and it's all over some dick that's going to be gone. You around here wasting your time."

"Bring your ass in this kitchen," Kenya said grabbing my arm tight as she pulled me down the hall.

"Get your hands the fuck off me," I said snatching out of her grip. Kenya backhanded me so hard I was seeing stars. If she wasn't my mom, I would have sliced her up.

"Why you put your hands on me?" I asked.

"Let me tell you something little girl. I don't owe yo' ass or anybody else a fucking explanation on who I'm seeing."

"You just said he was a friend but now you seeing him. You cheating on my dad," I said laughing.

"Queen if you forgot or can't see, you dad is gone. I'm still here on this earth and have needs. Don't get it twisted if your dad was here I would never have stepped out on him."

"I ain't tryna hear that bullshit," I cussed walking towards my room. Once I got in my room I went straight to my hiding spot.

"Where the fuck did my cash go?" I screamed as I looked at my empty hiding spot. There wasn't a single coin in there. I walked back out the room and found Kenya talking to Wes by the front door. He was leaving as he kissed Kenya on the nose and slapped her on the ass.

I was pissed off to no return.

"Where is my cash?" I demanded to know.

"I'll call you later boo," Kenya said to Wes as she closed the door behind him. She spun around with fire in her eyes, and said, "I used it."

"You spent it? All of it?"

"Yes… some stuff came up and I needed some extra money to handle it."

"What about my dope that was in there?"

"That's gone too."

I stormed back into my room to grab my bag.

"What are you doing back in Indianapolis anyway?" Kenya tried to talk to me but I shut the door behind me too fast to finish hearing what she was saying.

Chapter 19

"This whole time y'all bitches knew Kenya had some nigga all up in the house and it never crossed none of y'all minds to pick up the phone to shoot me a text to let me know," I asked walking up on the girls.

"Queen, come on lets take a walk. Don't be mad at the girls because I told them not to say anything," Aunt Marilyn said pulling me to the side. We took a walk over to the park on Udell.

"Listen, niece, she been chilling with dude for a few weeks now. I pulled up on him one day while Kenya was gone. I just didn't know how to tell you that type of shit so that's why I told the girls to stay out of it. At first I was mad hurt because I felt like she was disrespecting my brother and his house but Black Jesus is gone and she have to move on but that's only half of it. Now don't get mad at me but the streets been talking about Kenya talking about she's getting high now," Aunt Marilyn said dropping her head.

"Getting high off what," I asked.

"The same shit she been around our whole life?"

"Who saying this silly ass shit?" I asked.

"Bitch, everybody and they mom. They say she been going other places to get her dope because she knows nobody will serve her over this way."

My mind flashed back to my money and dope but I didn't understand it.

"I just want to update you on what's going on so you don't be blind to the facts. Everything's gone be a'ight niece," Aunt Marilyn said hugging me tight.

I appreciated Aunt Marilyn talking to me but fuck all that shit. We were talking about my mom. She couldn't fall off the boat because we were a money getting family. I was planning on staying at one of the girls house but with the new information I needed to be near my momma because whoever got her started on the dope was going to have to see me.

"Why you still holding on to that bag. What's in that bitch." Aunt Marilyn asked.

"I was planning on going over one of y'all house after seeing dude but it's only some clothes and shoes. I'm go put it up," I said as we walked back towards the block.

I went through the back door because I didn't want to see Kenya. Since her room was upstairs I knew she wouldn't see me coming in. I locked my room door. I dump the brick of heroine onto the table I had in my room, and tore the wrapper off. Grabbing one of my old masked I used when corona virus hit and some gloves before touching it. I looked at the color of the dope and it was the same as when she got her dope from Mookie. I went to work breaking it down to ounces and cutting it up. Then I broke down an ounce in all grams, and stashed the rest in foil and put it inside the freezer because I remember Cousin Pooder and Kenya told me something like it keeps it fresh. I changed into my black skinny jeans, black/red Jordan's and put on one of Black Jesus hoodies since it was suppose to be a little chilly outside. Then I went into Black Jesus' office to grab a gun out of his stuff. As I was tucking the .380 into the back of my pants, Kenya was walking passed but stopped at the door.

****

Inside a private suite in the Hilton Hotel, Big Jesus firmly had one of his lovers, Amber an F.B.I. employee, bent over the king-size bed. While he fucked her hard and rough from behind, she allowed her loud moans of ecstasy to escape throughout the suite.

"Do you love me," he yelled out.

"Yes! Daddy, I love you," she screamed.

"Will you do anything for me," he yelled again.

Yes, yes," she moaned as he continued to beat her pussy up. She had cum so much that she was seeing spots. She been fucking Big Jesus only for a few months but she was in love. She was giving him information that came through her office that would help him out. She knew the consequences behind dealing with Big Jesus but she didn't care.

After their sex session, Big Jesus cleaned up.

"Listen, my granddaughter is back in town so we need to get together sooner than later because I know she's going to be a problem. She's young but smart," Big Jesus said.

"Well we can't get her on one murder since we don't have anyone pointing any fingers so we gonna have to wait till she do something and then I can get her," Amber said kissing Big Jesus.

"Okay, let me figure something out."

****

"Queen is back on deck with them Black Jesus deals," I announced as soon as I stepped foot back on the block.

"You back on deck?" Porsche asked running her hands together.

"I only get excited when the pack touch down," I said pulling a fat gram out of my pocket.

Everybody jumped on them grams to the point I had to go back into the house three times. I sold 65 grams in the matter of an hour.

"Queen is that you?" CiCi asked, as I walked up to Roach. "Bitch where you been at these last few months?" She asked.

"Shit was hot out here so I had to deep off to Miami until shit cooled down. But all is good. I see you been keeping shit on lock," I said nodding to all the fiends up and down the block.

"Anyway, what's up with you, you been ok?" asked CiCi. She was sitting on the trunk of a BMW smoking on a blunt.

"I got them grams on deck," I said tossing her one to see.

"Hell yeah, I see you, let me get ten of those," she said digging inside her lone and pulling a wad of cash out.

"Queen got them Black Jesus grams!" CiCi announced. Everybody on the block rushed towards us trying to grab some. I sold out 35 grams and had an order for another 25 more.

I was back in my room sitting on the bed counting the money I just made. I had made ten thousand in two hours. I gave everyone my cellphone number so they could each me. I stashed my money, grabbed another 25 grams and hit the door. I was on my way to Duke since I haven't seen or talked to him in a few months. When I bent the corner I saw a group of niggas on his porch. Since it was getting dark out I knew they wouldn't be able to see me so I walked up the block.

"Who dat thick chick?" One of the dudes asked looking hard.

"Oh shit, Queen!" They all went crazy when I stopped in front of the house. Everybody came and showed me love except Money who stayed sitting on the stairs.

"What's all that noise?" Duke asked coming to the door.

"Queen!" he yelled, then ran out to give me a bear hug. "Why the hell a nigga couldn't get a call?" he asked.

"I'm sorry friend but I'm back now," I said.

"I'm glad cause these hoes and hoe ass niggas ain't on shit but selling other niggas shit. Where they do that shit at. We about to get to the bag," he said smiling.

"No doubt. That's one of the reasons why I'm over here to holla at you. You still tryna roll with me?"

"We can do that but we need a spot too so we can step our game up and fuck selling grams," Duke said.

I been around Duke for a long time so I knew he had game about himself.

"What's on your mind," I asked.

Duke pointed to an abandoned house we use to chill at and said, "We grab that house and open shop."

"Since Big Jesus has it sold up how we going to eat," I asked.

"You act like Big Jesus own this hood. The last time you had that work it was better than his so all we have to do is get different work then him and the fiends is going to come spend with us. Plus everybody know you Black Jesus' daughter so they would fuck wit you just behind that and you still can jump off the phone so we can corner the market," he said.

"It sound like you already been planning this come up," I said.

"I'm just tired of going backwards, Queen. Feel me?"

Ain't no reason why we are at the bottom and your Granddad and his crew at the top. Just because y'all blood you suppose to be good. That nigga ain't solid on the hood but I need you," Duke said.

"Let's get it cracking then," I said.

"Let me get a minute of your time," I said to Money as me and Duke walked up the stairs.

"What's up?"

"It ain't like that. I just want to clear the air and apologize to you. My mind was else place and when she grabbed my arm I just zoned out. I know you loved chick so my bad. Can you please accept my apology so we can move pass it?" I asked sincerely.

"I just didn't understand why you kept sizing her up," Money said.

"That something I bounce around in my head all the time. Anyway I wanted to say my piece and make sure we were coo because I did use to have a crush on you," I said smiling.

Money looked up at me with those pretty light brown eyes and smiled. "Yeah we good!"

Money stood and followed me inside Duke house where we continue to talk while smoking.

****

After spending a while over Duke's house me and Money came back to my house where we was alone for the first time ever. I couldn't believe it. It was like a dream come true. I had fantasized about him for so long. We were in my room listening to Rihanna's CD chilling on the bed. We had a blunt going back and forth. I hit a button that dimmed the light in the room. I was trying to get Money relaxed so I could get some dick from him. Every time I looked at Money's body my pussy jumped. Not being able to withstand the heat I jumped into his lap. When this fat ass landed onto his dick, it stood straight up. He began to kiss my lips and I swear I thought I was suckin honey. While still kissing me, he flipped my top over my head revealing my perfect round C-cups with light brown nipples. I tilted my head back from the feeling and let out a deep moan, as he took turns sucking both of my nipples.

I hopped up out of Money's lap and began to peel off my skinny jeans. I knew he was ready by how his dick kept jumping. He quickly got undressed then laid back on the bed. He pulled me towards him and lifted me up a little, helping me mount the head of his dick.

"Oh…" I sighed, as I slid down the base. I arched my back working my pussy muscles and threw my soft ass down on his dick like a vet that I was. He reached around gripping my ass cheeks bringing me up and down hard on his dick.

"Money," I moaned as I kissed his lips.

"Yeah baby," He whispered. His voice was low. I could tell he was ready to nut by the way his dick moved.

"Money... I'm coming...." I said. I knew he could feel my walls contracting. My body jerked as I continued to throw my ass on him while screaming.

"Ah...Ah...Oh my."

He dick exploded. "Ah" He groaned.

I have never felt a feeling that good before. I have had sex before with a few girls and a few dudes but what Money did to my body wasn't usual. I was out of breath and so was Money. I laid chest to chest with him with his dick still inside of me. I kissed him all over his chest until his dick got hard again and we were going for round two.

Chapter 20

One Week Later....

Everything me and Duke talked about in front of his house was in motion and it was going good. Duke had the spot jumping from sun up to sun down. Instead of selling grams for $100, Duke bust it down to points and was making $300 off each gram. I had already turned the brick into two so we had the best dope in the city. Nobody dope was better or bigger than ours.

Duke knew someone that made a stamp called Black Jesus and we stamped every point we sold. Duke ran the spot the same way his dad had his spot back when we were growing up. Since the hood rats was always around Duke's spot he put them to work. He paid for all the smoke, food and drinks but at the end of the day he gave them all $300 and they were okay with that.

Porsche had K-2 and Kush houses all over the city. Every house we opened up, we will have OG Ke-Ke from Udell come put up cameras and iron fences around the whole outside that way no one could get in or out unless we let them.

The only job I had was keeping the houses loaded with the dope. We only put a few ounces in the house at a time so that way we never took a big loss. I only dealt with Duke on the dope tip and Porsche would get her weed and put them into her houses. We all were doing good.

Most of the time I was in the house trying to just stack money without spending anything. I had put up $100,000 already but I remember Black Jesus telling me to always put something up for a raining day so I went back out back and buried $30,000.

Money was still going hard with his grind but he wanted me to give him all the dope so he could move it but I wasn't goin to sit back and let him control my money. He damn near moved into our crib. The only time I got out the house is when Duke or Porsche text me to meet them. Me and Money fucked all day. I haven't been spending anytime with the girls and I felt bad.

"Damn Money you lay that pipe down and got my niece all locked in the house saying fuck her girls?" Aunt Marilyn joked taking a seat.

"Nothing like that," Money said.

"Bitch when you going to come out and get some air?" Aunt Marilyn teased me.

"Please bitch." I laughed.

"Your birthday is around the corner, and ain't shit changed we always did it big so are we still on that," Aunt Marilyn asked.

"Hell yeah!" You know I have to do something silly."

"So we need to plan whatever you trying to do this year. We have to show up and out for the team. We have to let the lookers know we the hardest girl crew out here. And I know ya got a bag too since yo' spot been doing numbers around here. I even know Porsche behind all the K-2 and weed spots."

"What you talking about?" I asked

"So you goin sit in my face and play me like my ears ain't to the streets? While you in here getting piped down by Money you have Duke running the spot then Porsche got her cousin running her shop. Ain't nobody been doing this type of movement until you came back home."

"I hear you, but what you trying to do with this party? Let me know because I know you got something on your mind since you pulling up on me?" I said.

"Okay listen Pops said he will help us out so I was thinking about renting out C.J. Walker Theatre for the night for $10,000. The theater holds 7,500 seats. We out up the $35,000 Megan the Stallion want and another $20,000 for Stunna 4 Vegas. That's $65,00 but the thing is we can charge $100 a head making us $750,000 cash. Then we can put a few hundreds towards flyers and as you know our social media is already lit. We win all around feel me," Aunt Marilyn said.

My eyes was open wide listening to her break down the plan. I was with it when I heard $750,000.

"I know you with it by the look on your face," Aunt Marilyn said smiling.

"When this suppose to happen," I asked.

"As soon as we give Pops the money shit will be in motion for this weekend so we have a few days. I see you got your dream man." We both laughed.

"Bitch and the dick is something to kill for," I said getting up to get my half of the money.

When I walked back into the room Money and Aunt Marilyn were talking in low voices but stopped once they saw me.

"What y'all talking about," I asked handing her a bag with $33,000 on it.

"Oh nothing," she said leaving.

Chapter 21

All over social media they labeled me First Lady of the City. The party was the talk of the city. We had bitches hitting our Facebook we haven't talked to in years asking for free tickets. Our names were already in the streets but after reading the feedback I saw they were talking about us in other cities.

I wanted to send Money to the mall to grab us some outfits but I knew he would have us all in hood gear so I hit up Cousin Pooder and asked her to overnight me some clothes.

Cousin Pooder end up shipping this white Dior skit that hugged by body and some Caovilla sandals that wrapped up my thick legs. Of course I accessorized with diamond earrings Black Jesus gave me on my 15th birthday. I sported a gold Rolex on my wrist with a handbag.

Money sported a three piece Gucci suit with a thick gold chain with a Money sign in crush diamonds.

Together Money and I was going to shut the building down. Aunt Marilyn hired a few people to take our pictures when we arrived. We decided we wanted to be a little late. We also hired a driver for the night from Jacqueline Car Service. They picked us up from the house in a Bentley. It set me back $7,000 but it was worth it. Me and Money say back in the comfort of the car and enjoyed the ride as we slow cruised down MLK.

"Baby I want to say "Happy Soul Day," Money said grabbing my hand and kissing it. Then he presented me with a box.

When I opened it my eyes popped out of my face because I was staring at a $250,000 Franck Muller watch. I knew the cost because Black Jesus had one before.

"You like it baby?"

"Yes, Thank you Money."

****

There was a line that wrapped around C.J. Theatre that went two blocks long. All heads turned towards the **Bentley**, as the driver got out to open my door at the curb.

Flashing lights flicked as we pose for the camera at the top of the red carpet they had laid at the curb. Two big black bouncers met us at the door and led us inside. We just smiled as we heard on lookers talking about us.

"They just pulled up in a Bentley," one person said.

"Y'all see them diamond jumping," another one said.

When we stepped inside the building all ya heard was music blasting. We stopped and took some more pictures so everyone inside could get a good look at the hottest couple in the building. Aunt Marilyn did her thing to the theater. She had it to where V.I.P. was all the way up top. When I looked up I saw Trina waving for us to come up. We were led up some stairs that went up to the V.I.P section where everyone was at getting their party on. I went toward my girls and Money did the same.

"What up bitches?" I said walking up on the girls as they chilled.

"Bitch, you killin' 'em?" Aunt Marilyn said grabbing at my Dior skit.

"Happy Birthday, my bitch," Porsche said.

"We gone open up all your gifts later on but I want you to meet Megan the Stallion and Stunna 4 Vegas. They responsible for tonight," Aunt Marilyn said.

Stunna 4 Vegas just finished doing a few songs so Meg the Stallion was about to jump on the stage to do her thing. She hit her drink and escorted herself up to the stage. When she began her song Aunt Marilyn reached inside the bucket of ice that was sitting on the table and handed me a bottle of Raspberry Spritzer. She knew I liked my first drink. I popped the cork and hit bottled with the girls. We were all standing over the balcony dancing to the sound of Megan. The night was the best I have had in a while.

Me and Aunt Marilyn were getting love from all kinds of people in the game. Some of the people gave us their numbers and told us to get at them on some business.

Megan has did like three songs and was going to take a break for a while so she could chill so we all went down to the main floor to do our showing off for the haters.

Me and Money took a few pictures, stunting with twenty grand in blue face hundred dollar bills with "I Get Money" as the background. Then Duke and his tram did the damn thing, acting a fool. Then the crew flicked it up. Me, Aunt Marilyn, Trina, Porsche and Mercedes took our poses in front of "Loyalty is a Must" background and for some reason that background tug at my heart.

As we all linked back up to head up to out section, a little fight broke out. Aunt Marilyn and I were in the back talking so we couldn't really get a good look at who was fighting. The DJ shut the music off and told everyone to make room for the bouncers to get through but instead of making a way everyone started pushing and fighting each other.

Out of the blue I heard someone say, "You think you the baddest and then a punch hit the side of my head. Then another bitch tried snatching my handbag but she couldn't get her hand around it. I hit her with a two piece and a hook sending her back as Trina hit her in the back of the head making her go down to the floor. I spotted Aunt Marilyn going blow for blow with the girl that hit me first. I moved through the crowd in search of Money. I saw Porsche and Mercedes going to work on some bitch. Porsche had the girls hair while Mercedes went to work on her face.

"Boom! Boom! Boom!" gun shots ringed out, sending people in all type of directions trying not to get shot. When the crowd opened up I saw Monet looking at someone on the floor. I made my way towards were he was standing and saw Trina bleeding everywhere.

"No, No?" I said, not understanding what happen. The rest of the girls made it to where we was and watched Trina bleed from her chest.

"I see the light," Trina said, with a scared look in her eyes.

"Come on," I said grabbing Aunt Marilyn and Porsche by the hand.

"Who did this shit?" Porsche asked another female from the hood. She was standing there crying her eyes out, but managed to get it out, "Them bitches from 2-G."

We rushed out the exit door in search of them 2-G bitches. Soon as we got to the curb, some dudes pointed at two jeeps and said, "Them the chicks that fucked up the party."

I knew it was the chicks in the Jeep because we got into some of the same chicks at Riverside and plus one girl was hanging out the window throwing up 2-G and saying "We up one." I pulled by .380 from my handbag and started firing at the Jeeps as they began trying to speed down the block. One of the Jeeps slammed into a park car. I was in a zone to the point I was still firing after the clip was empty.

"Put the gun down," is all I heard in my ears but I was still in my zone. The cop fired a single shot that spinned me around and dropped me to the ground. I was laying in the street looking at the dark sky while bleeding. My whole body was hot and tears rolled down my cheeks as my ears were ringing loud.

"Hell Naw!" Money yelled trying to make his way towards me.

"Baby are you ok," he asked.

"Sir you need to stand back now," the cop said with her gun still in her hand.

Sirens and lights filled the block.

"Sir, you have to step back on the curb. The other police need to investigate what happen out here tonight," the female cop that shot me said to Money.

"Are you able to stand up because you don't have an exit wound so you were only nicked?" a black cop asked kneeling down next to me.

"Move?" an white cop told the black one then said, "Get to your feet because you going to jail," he said slapping cuffs on me.

Once I got to my feet a medic rushed over to me and checked my nick. The officer who had a hold of my arm then escorted me to a police cruiser that was at the curb. As soon as the door shut, the car sped off. I looked back and saw Aunt Marilyn and Money hugging. I knew I was about to go down.

Chapter 22

They took me downtown to the Processing Center and locked me inside a cell by myself since I was been charged for the shooting. I had yet to be told exactly what they were charging me with. I knew I got hit with the gun but I didn't know the outcome of the people in the Jeep.

"Queen Jesus, get ready," a officer told me as my cell door opened and a deputy stood there.

"Where am I going?" I asked.

"Come on there's some police here to talk to you," the deputy said.

An older female in the cell next to mines heard what the deputy said and came to the door and told me, "Keep your mouth shut and let them know you want a lawyer." I smiled letting her know I appreciated her. The deputy took me to this small room with a table and three chairs. There was two cops inside.

"Queen Jesus, is that it?" the female detective asked as I stepped in and took a seat.

"Yeah, that's my name why," I asked.

"Are you related to Black Jesus," she asked back.

That question made me sit up. After hearing my dad name I knew I was in trouble.

"What you say your name was," I asked the detective.

"My name is Amber."

"Well Amber, I want a lawyer please," I said.

"You hear this bitch, she wants a lawyer," Amber said to her partner smiling.

"You going to need a really good one to get you out of this jam so since you want a lawyer we going to be charging you with carrying a concealed weapon, attempted murder and murder."

"What you mean murder? I never murdered anyone," I said starting to sweat.

"Yes murder, its real. You going to be gone a long time because the Judge is going to give you the long haul. Help yourself out since you just turned 18 and you would be charged as an adult."

"Yeah I hear you. That's why I asked for a lawyer because I know the games y'all play," I said trying to keep my tears from falling and them seeing me sweat.

"Deputy take her ass back to the holding tank. We will see how your holding up in twenty five years," Amber partner yelled.

The deputy appeared at the door and escorted me back to the cell.

****

Nine o'clock the next morning I was awoken by a deputy screaming my name.

"Queen Jesus, court!"

I rushed over to the sink and washed my face as the door popped open.

"Keep your head up girl," the same woman next to me said.

I had to get chained up with about ten other girls and had to take a twenty minute walk underground until we made it to the part of jail where court be held. We were escorted to a filthy bullpen and the deputy told me, I was due in court at 10 o'clock. Everybody sat in the bullpen quite in their own thoughts on what was ahead for them. I knew Kenya heard the news by now and hired a lawyer but didn't understand why the lawyer haven't shown up to talk to me yet. I should have kept my ass in Miami I thought as I heard keys unlocking the bullpen.

"Queen Jesus," I heard. It was my lawyer, Mrs. Kid. I was so happy to see her.

"How's it going Queen?" she asked shaking my hand.

"I guess okay now," I said.

"When we go inside this courtroom let me work my magic and do all the talking. The charges your facing are serious. While you clocked up don't talk about your case to anyone."

"Okay."

"As of right now they're charging you with murder, attempted murder and carrying a weapon. Depending on what type of evidence, we may ask for a plea."

"How much time am I facing," I asked.

"Right now the murder holds from 40-65 years, the attempt murder holds 40 and they could give you 10 for the gun. But they'll come with a plea deal. Once the heat goes down on the case we will start talking then but that might take a few months so you will have to sit in jail until then. You're looking at about fifteen years worst case since you are so young," Mrs. Kid said looking at me.

"Fifteen years?" Damn I repeated. That sound so long. I'd be 33 years old. "I know we can do better than that."

"We're going to tell them we are going to trial that will give them time to come with a plea because they don't like spending money on trials. My experience in this game they going to offer something."

"Okay," I said dropping my head.

"It'll be okay," Mrs. Kid said patting my hand. "I'll see you in court."

"Is my mom is the courtroom," I asked.

"Yes, she's up there waiting."

****

The courtroom was packed. Every seat in there had someone sitting in it.

"We love you Queen!" Aunt Marilyn yelled out. She was seated in the front row next to Kenya, Porsche and Big Jesus. Most of the people there was from Da LAND and I guess the other people were the chicks in the Jeep families. I searched every inch of the courtroom looking for Money but he didn't show up to support me. I was looking forward to seeing his fine ass. I turned and looked at Kenya but she didn't look back at me and that told me a lot. She looked bad. Even though me and Money stayed in the house we kept our distance from her and did us. I felt really bad about keeping my distance and not talking to her because maybe I could have helped her get back to her old self. We needed each other more than not.

The Judge emerged from his chambers and read off the charges against me, which Mrs. Kid entered a not guilty plea on each charged. My next court date was scheduled for a month later, at which it would be determined whether the prosecutor had enough evidence against me to take it to trial.

"Preliminary hearing will be set for June 8th. There wouldn't be any bond at the moment. The defendant will remain in custody," the Judge said.

The prosecutor was all smiles as he talked to that cop Amber. He was a young dude maybe 30 something.

"Well Queen keep your nose clean until we come back to court."

I smiled at Mrs. Kid and that was the end. The court officer took me back to the bullpen with the rest of the ladies.

Chapter 23

Dec 8, Six Months Later...

For the past six months I sat downtown in the City County Building with all different types of women. I had a calendar and marked down everyday I stayed in that place hoping my lawyer would come in with some good news that would help me get home. When I first came back from court I told myself I would be home soon but that day yet to come. Mrs. Kid kept on trying to get me to sign a plea because she was only representing me at that point on the behalf of knowing Black Jesus so long. Kenya hadn't paid the last ten thousand on the lawyer bill and if I didn't take some type of plea I would spend the rest of my life in the white mans prison. She told me, she been trying to get ahold of Kenya but never reached her which I knew because I was in the same boat. She hadn't done anything since I been here.

Just like Mrs. Kid said she wasn't at my next court date so the court appointed me an attorney named Mr. Bones. The court was waiting on me to say yes or no to the plea deal.

"They waiting on your answer," Mr. Bones said.

"Okay I'll take the deal," I said putting my head down.

I just knew if I went to trial with Mr. Bones he would send me up the river. I was just hoping they showed me love today. The thing before Mrs. Kid hopped off my case she sent me a discovery of my case and it broke my heart to see Aunt Marilyn and Mercedes made a statement against me. They both was going to get on the stand for these white people.

Aunt Marilyn and Mercedes showed up on court. They kept smiling and waving at me. They didn't know I knew about them working with the prosecutor. The thing about them was they were sitting behind the prosecutor table. I didn't wave or smile back. I saw that Aunt Marilyn had a money sign on her neck like the chain Money had. I wondered what it meant.

Mr. Bones walked over to the prosecutor table said something then came back with the DA on his heels. The prosecutor looked down and me and said, "You have a few minutes to look over this plea but I'm telling you now if you don't sign it you will never see day light again on this side of the gate."

I read the plea two times until I knew I was satisfied because I wasn't going to sign my life away. They would drop the murder, attempted murder but the gun was staying. It said I couldn't get no more than ten years for the gun so I signed it.

Judge Miller shuffled some papers that laid on his desk.

"I would like to start by saying that I'm against this plea that's on the table today. If it was me, I would give you the max because with this plea it's no justices for the families. At the age your at and the crimes you committed shows me that your dangerous to our community but since the prosecutor want the plea I will accept the agreement."

"Do you understand the plea agreement Mrs. Queen?" Judge Miller asked.

"Yes, You Honor. I read over it twice," I said

"Very well then. Would the prosecutor proceed on the plea," Judge Miller asked.

"Thank you for accepting the plea and were asking for sentencing today," the prosecutor said.

Just like that all the charges were dropped except the gun. The families were furious at the deal. They had put police officers throughout the courtroom just in case something happened.

"You are able to speak before getting sentenced," Mr. Bones said.

"Yes I would love too," I said standing. "I would like to say I know my mother isn't here today but I want to tell her sorry for taking her through this mess. And to my ex auntie and friend, I want y'all to know I read it," I said before sitting back down.

"Very well then. I am ready to impose sentencing at this time. I am sentencing you to the custody of Indiana Department of Correction for six years. Court is adjourned."

"You don't have to do all that time if you get down there and get some time cuts plus keep your nose clean," Mr. Bones said as the court officer rushed me out of the courtroom. I looked at Aunt Marilyn and Mercedes and just shoot my head.

Chapter 24

Rockville Correction facility read the sign. The van had to go through three gates. The ride wasn't that long from Indianapolis. No one in the van spoke the whole ride, I guess we all were in our thoughts. I had heard stories about prison plus I use to see a show called Lockup. I knew if people didn't stand on their ten toes they were food.

As soon as we got off the bus we were rushed inside to intake. They lined us up against the wall while they uncuffed our shackles and chains. We had to walk through a series of electronic sliding doors. After each door it felt like I wasn't never going home. When we were done getting strip down they gave us clothes, hygiene, laundry bag and mat all state issues.

****

"New people coming!" Someone yelled, as me and two other females walked in the unit.

We all stood at the officer desk waiting on her to tell us what room we were assigned to. Even though my back was facing the unit I could feel everybody eyes on me.

"Jesus you're in cell 224 lower," the officer said pointing to some stairs that led to the second range. When I took the stairs it was like ten females just standing there mugging me looking like niggas.

"Queen!" a voice yelled out. I looked up and saw a face from the hood.

"Sade, what's up girl?" I said excitedly to see someone I knew.

"Y'all bitches better move out the fucking way and let my sister up them stairs before it be a problem." Sade ordered.

Them bitches parted like pussy lips.

"What room you in?" asked Sade.

"Okay, you're in there with this lame chick named Ashley. Come on let me take you down there so you can see this bitch. She's one of them upped bitches. She think her shit don't stink so I had to put my hands on her a while back," Sade said.

Sade was from Edgemont and had two brothers that had the streets scared at one point.

"Ashley, this is my sister Queen from the city. She's in this cell with you until we can get her somewhere else," Sade said.

The chick Ashley never looked up as she wrote a letter on her jail issue tablet. She was a black pretty chick with long hair.

"Bitch, I know you hear me talking to you?" Sade snapped. Sade had put on a little weight making her thicker.

"It's coo with me, I'm not tripping," Ashley said.

Chapter 25

Sade had gained a reputation at Rockville, she had beat up a lot of females who tired her. She grow up in the house full up boys so her hands was the truth. If a bitch was standing on all she talked about Sade would let it be known. She never sugar coated shit. The whole prison respected Sade and what she stood for. Since I walked through the door it was me and Sade. People knew we were sisters so they showed me love. Sade made sure I had everything I needed. I haven't even been to commissary and my locker was filled up with all type of food, hygiene and clothes. She even got me a 15' flat screen T.V. It fucked me up when I saw females paying her for safety.

I been at the prison for a few months now and no one from the outside world got at me. My heart hurt because I haven't done anything but show people love when I was out there but I see when its out of sight out of mind.

Me and Sade was now cellies. I would start stressing and Sade would get me at me. She told me to cut out the outside world because it would make my bid easy. Everyday Sade made me get up and worked out with her. She told me I had to keep in shape in case someone tried me.

"Sade" is all you heard when we walked through the door of the cafeteria. They were on my girl's pussy hard. Not too many people knew my name besides the few Sade told. I grabbed a tray and got me so food. We headed to the Indiana part of the cafeteria. This female Tasha bumped Sade as we walked to our table.

"Watch were you going," Sade said.

"Naw you watch your steps," Tasha said getting loud.

"Don't try me, bitch," Sade said walking up to Tasha.

"You see a bitch hit her in the mouth," Tasha said and that's just what Sade did hit her in the mouth. Everybody started fighting. I slapped some bitch with my tray of food and started beating her ass but stopped when I saw Tasha with a knife headed in Sade direction. I ran over and began stabbing her all in her back. I wasn't trying to kill her but wanted her to know not to fuck with my people. Someone stabbed me in my side sending me to my knees.

"Get down on the ground!" Nobody listened to the police and kept on fighting.

"Boom! Boom! Boom!" they let off gun shots then they came running in. Blood was everywhere. Four up North bitches were dead and two Indiana ones. I had blood coming out of my back like water. They had to rush me to the nurse. They told me if whoever done this went a little deeper I would have died.

Chapter 26

For the past month the whole prison been locked down for what happen in the cafeteria. They had sent Sade and Tasha to the hole since the snitches pointed the finger at the two.

Sade had sent me a kite letting me know that the administration didn't want to let her out because she had too much power so she would be finishing her bid on the hole. She told me to keep everything in the room because even in the hole she was good. I was pissed off because Sade was the only person I dealt with. I didn't fuck with the rest of these hoes. Sad I sat down thinking about Kenya and my crew so I started writing a letter something I wasn't use to. I knew if I wanted to finish my bid I had to stay busy by getting into some programs. One thing Sade told me was you can't stress over things you can't control.

While the prison was on lockdown I started reading a lot of books and planning my goals for when I touched down. The city was going to feel my pain. I continued to workout everyday and when the prison lift the lockdown I signed up for school and every job until they gave me one been a tutor. I scored so high on my test they told me, I could be a tutor and do school at the same time.

Females around the prison started saying "Hey Queen! What's up girl?" Whenever we crossed paths. Word around the prison was I held it down for the team and even took a stab in the process. I was eating good, working out everyday so I was thicker than a snicker now. I had not one ounce of fat on my body. I had a few females come on to me but I turned that down fast.

After year in half been locked up a letter came through the mail with Kenya's name on it. The scent from the letter was her Prada Candy.

Dear Queen:

I'm sorry you just now hearing from me. It hurt me to see you like that. I'm going through so much pain. As a mother, I know I have done wrong by taking so long to get in touch with you. I'm all alone out here and wish you were here by my side like you suppose to be. I really love and miss you. I hope you are doing ok in there. Don't give them girls to much pain. LOL. Get them time cuts and get back out here. Everything's the same out here. The hood is gone be the hood. Your crew out here doing they thing. Porsche comes by everyday to check on me. She ask about you all the time. I put some money in your account most of it came from Porsche. I love you Baby girl.

Kenya

I grabbed a pen, paper and a picture I took a few weeks back and sat at the table in my room.

Dec 14, 2015

Dear Kenya:

How you out there holding up? I hope all is well on that side of the gate if not just keep pushing it. I been holding it down in a good way. All I do is workout, read, go to school and work my job. I'm trying to knock this time down the best way I can. Listen you didn't raise me to be fake so I'm not going to start bow. I know that dope has a hold of you and that's one of the reason you turned your back on me. I been locked up for a year in half and this my second time hearing from you. I want to hate you but I can't. I love you and hope you do get it together because that dope isn't suppose to have you like fuck me. Tell Porsche I said I love her and she's doing what solid bitches do. Well you take care of yourself out there and know I love you.

Queen

****

May 19, 2020

Sic years later since I been locked up. I did my whole bid without any help. I stood tall all by myself. At first my time was slow because all I could do was thinking about the streets. Once I got into school and school a job my time went by fast,

Everybody at Rockville knew my day was coming because I ran a store so I had so much food and fed the whole dorm every night up until the night before.

I say in receiving and discharge for an hour waiting on my papers to get through, then I could leave. When I stepped out into the sun and screamed. The guard who was driving me to downtown Indianapolis was just shaking his head. I was no longer a young girl but a grown woman that was about to turn 24 in a few days. I couldn't wait to get back to the city and dig up my break. The whole time we were riding back to the city I couldn't stop smiling.

There was no more lock ins, chow time or having to shit in the room with someone else. I was a free bitch now. I didn't know what laid ahead when I got home. It had been years since I heard from anyone. I'm starting from the bottle but the money I had buried would give me a start.

****

The guard pulled in front of the mall downtown. Me heart was doing flips as I got out of the van. My smile was so big

I knew everyone that walked past could see every tooth in my mouth.

Damn, it felt good to be back in the city. People were moving around like they didn't have a care in the world.

"Hello, do you know what time it is," some dude asked me.

"No, I just got out of prison so no phone or watch," I respond with a smile.

"Me too. I did ten years, he said and you.

"I did six and some change."

I began to walk to the bus stop because I knew they came every hours and I didn't want to miss it.

"Take care of yourself," dude said.

I had about $1,625 that I kept on my books so they gave me a card with it on there and a bus pass. When I stepped onto the bus it was packed. I messed me up that the ride on the bus cost $3 now.

I got off the bus on 29th MLK because I wanted to take in the good air and get my head right just in case shit was fucked up at home.

Chapter 27

"Hey, Porsche, who is that bitch walking up to Kenya house?" asked Mercedes. Her and Porsche was standing beside an Infiniti truck.

"Bitch like I suppose to know. She can't be from around here wearing them knock off Timberland boots," Porsche said passing the blunt to Mercedes.

****

My heart dropped in my stomach as I walked up into the yard of our house. I couldn't believe my eyes, there was an old rusted car in the middle of the yard with trash surrounding it. I shook my head as I knocked on the front door.

"Come in," a voice said.

When I walked into the house smoked slapped me in my face. I covered my nose making sure not to inhale any smoke. Kenya had let the house go to waste, there were dope fiends all through the house smoking or shooting up dope.

"Who are you?" A woman asked looking at me all crazy and shit.

I didn't answer right away.

"Hello, you looking for somebody?" asked the woman.

"Yeah, I'm looking for Kenya." I said still not believing how the house looked.

"She'll be back soon," the woman said continuing to do her dope like I wasn't standing there.

****

"On your stomach," Big Jesus demanded. Kenya flipped on her stomach and slid her right hand under her and fingered her soaking wet clitoris.

"I like when you play with your pussy for me," Big Jesus whispered in Kenya's ear.

Kenya knew the right things to get Big Jesus off. She hate what she became. Big Jesus entered Kenya's pussy with force.

"OH! Hmmm…Hmm," Kenya moaned, while Big Jesus went in and out of her. "Right there! Harder! Harder!" Kenya pleaded as Big Jesus grabbed a hand full of her dreads.

"Who's pussy is this?" he grunted pumping in and out with force without a care in the world.

"It's your puss—eee-e-e!" Kenya yelled as Big Jesus shot his cum all inside her pussy,

"Here," he said throwing Kenya a gram of heroin. She was so in a rush to get high she didn't even wipe the cum off her leg as it dropped out of her pussy. She grabbed the dope off the floor and went to her pipe.

Big Jesus walked out the backroom into the living room where he saw a thick chick standing there,

"Damn, who are you," I heard a voice behind me. Even though it had been years I knew that voice from anywhere. When I turned around Big Jesus eyes popped out of his face.

"Queen?" he said looking at me.

"What up Pa?" I said cracking a smile.

"Girl you better give me a hug," he said rushing over to where I stood and lift me off my feet in a bear hug. "Baby girl you have put on a few pounds but you look good with it?"

"Yeah I know."

"Kenya! Get your ass in here," Big Jesus yelled. "Kym, ya remember my grandbaby. She done got older and bigger,"

Big Jesus said to the woman that told me to come into the house.

I looked at the woman and couldn't believe my eyes because the last time I saw her, she was a bad bitch and now she just look like something off the walking dead show.

"Hey Queen," she said smiling with two front missing teeth.

"What's up?" I said.

"What's going on out here?" Kenya asked walking into the room but stopped in her tracks when her eyes laid on me standing there.

"Is that my baby?" she asked crying.

"Everybody out my house now," Kenya screamed.

"I'm let y'all talk for a while but I will see you later," Big Jesus said to me.

We stood in the living room just looking at each other and it hurt me to see what my mom had become. She was once on top of the world but the woman that stood before me was a dope fiend.

"So I guess this is the new you?" I said.

Kenya just stood there crying. "Baby I missed you so much. I'm glad your home," she said.

"You missed me huh. Is that why I never saw you or talked to you my whole bid. Look at what you done to the house. This the only thing my daddy left you and you trash it like fuck him, I see," I said starting to get mad.

If Kenya wasn't my mother, I would have put my hands on her for disrespecting my father.

"I'm sorry, Queen," she said still crying.

"Fuck all that shit. Starting today you going to tell your dope fiend friends this isn't a hang out anymore," I said walking towards the front door.

When I opened the door Porsche stood there looking at me with a smile on her face.

"Bitch, what's up?" she said.

"Hey bitch, I missed you so much," I said happy to see my best friend.

"Our crew is back together," she said as I watched Aunt Marilyn and Mercedes walk up in the yard.

"What up bitch?" Aunt Marilyn said as she tried to hug me.

I stepped back and looked at her like she was crazy.

"Fuck you on bitch?" Aunt Marilyn asked.

"Neither one of you bitches got at me. Porsche the only one that sent money and checked on Kenya."

"Bitch you know how the game is. We were thinking about you though," Mercedes said.

"Were y'all thinking about me when y'all were going to help them white people send me up the river by getting on the stand. My lawyer sent me, my discovery before she hopped off my case and I read everything y'all told them people," I snapped.

Porsche stood next to me and looked at both of them.

"Y'all two bitches are the reason I went to prison because of them fucking statements," I said.

"What?" Porsche said, looking at them with fire behind her eyes.

"Tell me you're playing Queen?" Porsche asked not wanting to believe that the two people she looked at like sisters was the reason the crew broke up.

"Let her know y'all told the police I was the shooter and made y'all come with me," I said.

"Bitch you were the one that was out there shooting like you wasn't already on the run. We never told you to shoot them people. I wasn't going to go to prison for the rest of my life for some shit you did so in the end it was me or you and I'm going to always pick me first," Aunt Marilyn said.

"Y'all bitches can get to stepping matter face," I said.

"I got your bitch. I don't know who you think you talking to but I run shit," Aunt Marilyn said,

"Ain't shit changed. I'm still that bitch and always will. My hands are grade A. Yeah we older but I can look into your eyes and see you scared of me," I said,

"Y'all need to chill out," Porsche said.

I looked at Mercedes who took a stand behind Aunt Marilyn. I knew Aunt Marilyn could fight but I was just more skilled.

"You up one," Aunt Marilyn said, waving Mercedes peon ass to follow as she began to walk across the street. Before she could get all the way she stopped and looked at Porsche and said, "If you not coming with us make sure you stay on that side."

"Bitches, y'all already know who I'm with. You two are rats and I would never fuck with y'all again," Porsche said.

"You know it will never go back to the way it used to be with them doing that to me," I said seating on the porch.

"Bitch you know you my sister for life and I would have rode out with you. I will never cross you a day in my life," Porsche said.

"I know you won't because we cut from the same cloth, but why didn't you come and see or write me bitch," I asked.

"To tell you the truth I don't know. I was out here trying to stay above water. I came to check on Kenya and gave her my last few bands to pay for your lawyer," Porsche said putting her head down.

"Damn I didn't know that was how she paid the lawyer. She did write and let me know you were stopping by so thank you. I guess you got a bag now after all this time," I said.

"Bitch the only person getting that bag is Marilyn. She have the hood on lock and everybody scared to go against her. Anyway here's some money," she said handing a stack. "If I'm not mistaking your soul day is in a day or two so what you want to do?" she ask.

"I'm not even worry about my soul day, I'm trying to put a plan together to get this bag and then I will celebrate it," I said.

"Damn that nigga fine as hell," I said watching a dude come out of Big Jesus house.

He was walking with a little boy about the age of four and a little girl about two years old as he walked to the Infiniti truck that sat in front of the house.

"That's his car," I asked.

"Girl I told you Marilyn has shit on lock. That's one of her cars."

"Why he ain't driving his own car," I asked.

"Bitch him and your auntie started fucking around like two months after you got locked up. They have two kids. Marilyn left for almost a year and came back with they don, you see tight here then she dropped they daughter," Porsche said.

Porsche fucked my head up with that shit. I had flashbacks of them talking in the room and then when I saw in the back of the cop cars. They probably been fucking all along. We sat there talking about everything that had been going on in Da Land.

Chapter 28

"Queen if you ever need something make sure you get it on your own. I gave you the game so you didn't have to depend on anybody. You know I named you Queen because I knew you came from a long line of them. But remember every Queen needs a King by her side so find someone you know I would approve of. Sit in my chair Queen. Now you see this controller that control the chair," Black Jesus asked.

"Yes daddy," I answered.

"Okay if something every comes up and I'm not here or your mother press these two buttons at the same time and this little wall will pop out and there will be some money in there. Don't be just spending it because it's there," he said.

My eyes popped open and I rushed into my daddy's office. His chair was old and tore all up but I sat in it and pressed the two buttons. Nothing happen so I checked the remote which didn't have any batteries so I went and grab some fresh ones and tried again and the wall opened up. I couldn't believe my eyes. The wall had stacks of money filled to the top of it. I shit the office door and just stood there smiling. I found a old dirty sheet laying in the corner and started dropping the money in it. Since Kenya's room was upstairs I didn't have to worry about her. It took me two trips to get all the money to my room where I locked the door. It was two envelopes address to me and Kenya.

****

Dear Queen:

Baby girl is you're reading this letter that means I'm not there and I'm sorry. I told you a long time ago how to get this money because I knew you would do something with it. Your mom would have just spent it on any and everything she could. Do what you have to do to make sure you and your mother is okay. Me and your granddaddy been having problems so keep an eye on him because nine out of ten he's the reason I'm not there. Don't forget family is who you make it to be. Kiss and hug your mom for me. I love you.

-Dad-

As I read the letter Black Jesus wrote I seemed like he was standing in front of me. I was going to hold onto Kenya's letter until the right time. I wiped my face and began to count the money. Black Jesus already had the money in stacks in amount of $10,000. I put them in five stack piles coming up with $500,000. I couldn't believe it. I already had plans on what I was going to do. Plus I still had $30,000 I was going to play with. I put the money back up and laid across my bed while me mind wandered.

Chapter 29

I was up and out the door a little past 8:45 a.m., and I knew the mall opened up around 9:00-9:30 a.m. I called a uber and waited outside the house for the car to pull up. I was on my way back downtown to the mall which was only ten minutes away. I already had Porsche use her cash app to pay for the uber so when the car pulled up I jumped in. The uber driver was an older man blasting Lil' Baby.

When we pulled in front of the mall I hand the uber driver a big face hundred and told him to wait for me.

"You too young to have old hundreds like this," he said.

"Yeah I been saving every dollar since I was a little girl. I still got my lunch money from the third grade," I said jumping out.

"Hey, here's my number just text me when you're ready to move around," he said screaming his number through the window.

When I walked into the mall I went straight to the Gucci store on the second floor.

"May I help you?" this white lady asked me as I stepped through the door.

"Yes I need some dresses, skits and heels in size 6," I read off my size. She just stood there looking at me crazy.

"I said what I need so do I have to take this twenty thousand to another store," I said pulling money out of my bag.

The woman rush through the store grabbing outfits for me to try on. Most of the stuff was cute so I tried them on. I put this Gucci dress on that hugged my body like a glove and some heels to watch. We went right to the register so I could get out of there.

"That'll be $10,275.16," she said.

"That's it for all these outfits? You can keep the change," I said handing her the money.

I went up to a floor to Finish line to grab me some Air Maxes, Jordan's and some Air Force Ones. Coming out the store there was a spirit store right there so I went to grab a phone. I texted the uber driver from my new iPhone. When I walked outside he was at the curb waiting on me.

"You done?" he asked getting out to help me with my bags.

"Where we headed to now?" he asked.

"I need some wheels but nice ones," I said passing him a few more hundred dollar bills.

He looked at the money then me and said "I got the perfect spot."

When we pulled into the car lot my eyes locked in on this all black and red Bentley Continental Convertible.

"That's a bad bitch," I said climbing out of the uber rushing over to look at it. The tag said $65,000. It was a 2012 but looked brand new.

"You trying to spin the block in it?"

I turned around to face the man talking. He was a young fine brother with deep waves. He was dressed in a tailor suit with some Gucci loafers on, and he sported an plain Rolex which told me, he had some money because he didn't try hard.

"Hell yeah, I would love too," I said smiling.

"Do you have a license?" he asked.

"No," I almost stuttered.

"It don't matter. Just don't hit anything," he said waving for me to get in.

I put my seat belt on and hit the road. It was so smooth that I was scared to open her up. After a few blocks I was in love and had to have it.

"I got $55,000 cash for her," I said pulling back into the car lot.

"Deal?" He said smiling.

"I will handle all the paperwork just bring the $55,000 but since you don't have a license I'm going to need another $10,000 to get you one."

It took me twenty minutes to get there and back.

"I'm ready," I said taking a seat in the man's office.

"Well sign here and there. Now on paper it looks like you are making payments but the car is yours. Let's take a picture for your license then you would be ready to ride out," he said.

When I got back outside the uber was smiling.

"Nice doing business with you young lady," he said.

I cracked up "Black Youngsta" song called Beef and put it on repeat. I was dancing as I pulled up to the light. When the light turned green I could have swore I saw Sade riding pass in a new BMW so I caught up with the car at the next light.

"Sade," I said jumping out of the car at the light to go hug her.

"Girl when you get home?" She asked me.

"Yesterday."

"And you doing it big already. That's yours?" she asked Looking at the car.

"Yeah girl fuck this when you get home?" I asked.

"I been out for a while. I'm just working, taking care of my kids ya feel me?"

"Well I'm home now we about to put it together. I'm going to follow up and you hop in with me," I said peeling off leaving Sade behind.

Chapter 30

It was the perfect scene for me. The block was packed, sun out and people partying out there. When me and Sade turned down 28th I turned up "Black Youngsta" Beef letting the car creep.

"My bitch stunting out here," Porsche shouted when I pulled up and stopped at the curb. I jumped out Gucci down, knowing I was a bad bitch. Everybody on the block stopped what they were doing and just stared at me. The kids ran up to the car to touch it.

"Bitch, you hell," Porsche said giving me a hug.

"You been knowing that. I had to pop out on these hoes," I said.

"I knew you were holding because we were making a little noise before you went in. And the fact you never asked Marilyn about that money y'all made from the party put the cherry on top," Porsche said.

"You remember Sade," I said.

"Yeah. Hey girl," they both spoke.

"Sade showed me love as soon as I walked through the doors of that prison."

"Them bitches face dropped when you just pulled up? You auntie spit her drink out," Porsche said.

"We about to turn the heat up around here. They ain't never seen any bitches get money the way we bout to get it. I need both of y'all know I would put my life in y'all hand because y'all had showed me what lie in y'all heart already. Y'all two know of each other but don't know each other.

Please for me I'm going to take this trip out of town because the way I'm about to turn up I need Kenya away from here. She needs to get clean so go out and have fun because when I come aback it's go time," I said handing both of them bands.

When I walked into Kenya's room she was sitting on the bed.

"You still upset with me Queen. I can't stand that look in your eyes when you look at me. I'm ready to get clean. It hurt me hard when you said what you said about Black Jesus. It hit home," she said.

"Momma, I love you and sort that I spoke to you that way. I just hate to see you the way you are and since you ready to get clean then I'm ready to help you with that. I want you to read this letter, I said kissing her the same way Black Jesus did.

"What letter, red it for me," she said lying back on the bed.

"Okay."

Dear Kenya:

If you reading this letter that means Queen gave you this letter for me. I ant you to know that I will always love you and not a soul can take that away. When I first looked into your eyes, I knew you were going to be my wife and when you gave me Queen, you made me the most happiest man twice in one lifetime. I know I'm not there and I'm sorry but I need you to remain the strong woman I married for not only Queen but for yourself. Queen going to take good care of you because we raised her. Well I have to go love you baby.

Black Jesus –

"How?" Kenya asked crying harder.
"Don't worry mom," I said.

Chapter 31

After leaving Kenya's room I went back into my room and laid across the bed. Sade and Porsche cut out. I didn't know how I was going to help Kenta get clean since she's always around dope fiends.

Scrolling through social media I ran across cousin Pooder page. I sent her a message with my number explaining about me and Kenya. I told her to have cousin Punkin call me. No more than ten minutes late a 305 number called and it was cousin Punkin. I haven't talked to her in years. I explained to her everything that been going on and the first thing she said was "Send me Kenya."

****

I got online and got me and Kenya two first class tickets to Miami. I told Kenya to leave everything from then on she was going back to the old Kenya so she didn't need anything reminding her of her old life. I had Sade give her momma $10,000 so she could transfer $150,000 out her business account to cousin Pooder business account just so I will have money on standby just in case I'm able to connect some dots. I made sure to keep track of every dollar I spent. So far I was doing good. We made it onto the plane and I watched Kenya look out the window.

"When you get back it's going to be like you never left or went through anything but I don't want you to forget that you're loved," I said.

"Thank you for supporting me, Queen it means a lot to me," Kenya said wiping tears from her eyes.

When we came strolling out the airport cousin Punkin, cousin Pooder and they driver stood on the curb waiting for us.

"There they go," I said pointing.

"Kenya, Punkin," they both said at the same time as they bust out in a sprint towards each other.

"Look at you cuz. You done fell down but we going to lift you back up," Punkin said.

"Hey cuz," cousin Pooder said hugging me.

"Come on, let's get outta here," Cousin Punkin said, leading the way to a brand new Porsche truck.

"This is cute, cousin," I said as I sunk into the white leather seats.

"You know I have to stay fresh," Cousin Punkin said she her driver pulled into traffic.

Cousin Pooder sat up front while me, Kenya and cousin Pooder sat in the back. They were back there telling old stories. It been years since they saw each other. I overhead Black Jesus and cousin Pooder's dad Uno's name come up a few times. Puttin pieces together I understood Uno has the city on lock and use to hit Black Jesus off with bricks. They crew was called "West-Side Family."

****

"Damn Punkin, this y'all house? Y'all got down here and turned up on these down south bitches," Kenya said as we pulled up cousin Punkin's driveway.

"Yeah, cuz. I'm doing alright. My house is always yours so stay as long as you like and you welcome to anything inside," Cousin Punkin said as her maid opened the door for us.

Walking through the front door I went straight to my old room with cousin Pooder on my heels. The room still had all my old clothes inside and that surprised me. Some of the clothes still had tags on them. I was too big for them now. I hopped on the phone and hit Sade to check on her and to see if the transfer went through yet.

Cousin Pooder checked her account and let me know everything was all good.

"We need to go shopping," I said to Cousin Pooder.

"That pink Porsche is mines, you take it because I have to be at work soon," she said tossing me the key. "Pick out something nice because mom is having a get together tonight. Also here's that money," Cousin Pooder said opening a safe and laying stacks on the bed.

Chapter 32

I never even sat in a Porsche before let alone drive one. The truck had power and I was loving it as I zoomed in and out of traffic on my way to see if Tiffany stayed in the same house. Her dad stayed in a big house about three blocks from cousin Punkin years ago. When I pulled in front of the house it still looked the same. It was two BMW's in the driveway. By the time I was walking up to the porch Tiffany was coming out the house.

"Who you want?" Tiffany asked looking at me. I know I had gain a little bit of weight but I still looked the same. Yes it been some years but I never forget a face, maybe a name. Tiffany had long dreads now and a nice shape. You could tell she worked out a lot.

"Damn girl it's me Queen," I said smiling.

"Bitch what up," Tiffany said hugging me tight. "Look at you. You all thick and shit. I missed you so much."

"Yeah I thought of you too. I came to see if y'all still stayed here and to see if you was ok. You will always be my sister for life. I felt so bad for dipping out on you when we went on that trip but I couldn't help it," I said.

"Girl I already knew you were going to do that because I would have did the same thing myself," she said laughing.

"Yeah I had to get back to Indianapolis because that's all I knew."

"What you doing back in Miami?" Tiffany asked taking a seat on the lawn chair on the porch.

"Listen I'm going to be honest and not sugar coat shit. I need your help on something," I said looking at her.

"Talk to me."

"Well I have a problem back at the crib. I need a plus bad because I'm trying to turn the heat up in the city. Do your pops still be doing his thing?" I asked.

"Girl, that nigga will never give that shit up. You see them BMW's they both mines and I own two cribs fucking with him. What you trying to get plugged into?"

"I need a little of everything," I said.

"Don't trip I go speak with Pops now since he's in the crib chilling," she said walking inside the house.

"Queen," I heard my name. I saw Tiffany waving me to come into the house. I followed her into the basement where her dad was watching a football game.

"Hello young lady," Tiffany dad said looking at us.

"Dad you remember my friend Queen that rode back to the city that one time?" Tiffany asked.

"Yeah I remember her. You were crying for weeks behind her," He said laughing.

"How you doing, sir?" I said smiling at his comment.

"Stop that sir that's for my dad. You still can call me Roast. So what's up? Tiffany tells me you in the game now and looking for a plug. If you not talking right you can walk yourself back out that door. I don't do small shit either," Roast said.

"Nah I wouldn't disrespect you," I said.

"So, what you need?"

"I need to know how much bricks of heroin cost first," I said hoping he give me a good deal.

"Well since you are my daughter's friend I will give it to you for $35,000 a piece and sweetheart that's a good deal."

"If that's the case I want four bricks. You have that for me?" I asked.

"Four bricks really small but I got you. That will be $140,000. You big time like that to the point you can drop $140,000 like that?" he asked me.

"Hold tight," I said rushing out the house to the truck. "This is $150,000 right here. I know you can get me some points of K-2 (synthetic weed)," I said.

"Okay that's four bricks and twenty pounds of K-2. But the thing is getting it back to Indianapolis," he said.

"How much would that cost me to get that there for me?"

"Give me another $10,000 and I for you, young lady."

"I will have it waiting for you when touch down in the city with the shit."

"You going to have to give me a few days to make that drop. You can meet me where you dipped out on us at. You better not be late," he said.

"Okay, you can take it three days because I have a few moves to make here in Miami before I get back to the city but here's my number. Just text me and I will be there waiting on you," I said.

I was all smiles as me and Tiffany walked back outside.

"Girl you just made my dream come true," I said.

"It's nothing I won't do for a sister and plus I get a cut of that money. I been thinking about coming back to the city and chill with moms for a few months," Tiffany said.

"Hell yeah while you there we can get this money together if you down. I have two solid sisters that you would love," I said smiling.

"Fuck it I'm down," Tiffany said.

I had a few more hours to go until Cousin Punkin get together started.

****

Tiffany took me to some upscale boutiques so we could do some shopping. I told her about the party. We copped some outfits, heels shades and a few bags. I did a little shopping for Kenya as well.

Cousin Punkin's house was in full swing when I pulled into the driveway. I carried my bags inside the house but when we stepped in people were everywhere. Two fine brothers eyed us as soon as we stepped in.

"Let us help you pretty ladies with these bags," one said as both started grabbing them out of my hands. The took the bags into the other room and came back to talk to us. We sipped on a bottle of Assyrtiko since that's all cousin Punkin had out. They said she had her maid cook up fish, roast chicken and pork for those who wanted it.

"Queen you been gone almost all day," Cousin Punkin said as her and Kenya walked into the room.

Looking at Kenya at that moment you would never knew she was just doing dope days ago. Cousin Punkin cleared her up nice.

"Yeah I had to handle some business and clear my head. I had to pick up my sister," I said pointing at Tiffany.

"Hello, I'm Tiffany."

"I remember Queen telling me about you. I'm cousin Punkin and this is Queen's mom, Kenya," cousin Punkin said.

This fine brother walked through the front door while we were talking. His Polo outfit showed off his muscles. He started walking towards us looking like money. I locked in on him and to my surprise it was Nelly. I got up from the seat I was in and met Nelly halfway.

"Hey Nelly," I said.

"Hello. Do I know you?" he asked.

"It's Queen boy," I said smiling.

"Oh shit. Come here and give me a hug," Nelly said finally recognizing me.

"Boy you better drop hugging me like that," I said.

"You still looking good Queen. To be honest you look better and got thick," Nelly said looking at my body.

"Thank you. It has been six plus years," I said.

"Let's go some place and chop it up," Nelly said grabbing a glass of wine.

We headed outside so we could be alone and talk. We sat at a table that had a bucket of ice on it that had a bottle of Aperitivo Do Torino inside.

"What you been up to all these years Queen?"

"Well when I went back home I got into a little trouble and ended up doing six years in prison. I'm just coming home a few days ago," I said.

"I'm glad you okay. You should have reached out to me or Punkin because we would have held you down. I asked Punkin about you a few times and she blew it off," he said.

"Enough about me. How you been doing?" I asked.

"I have my own business that makes chips for new cards. I been doing good but trying to connect the dots through Punkin."

"It's good to see you," I said.

"Same here,"

We just stared at each other for a minute. We both was feeling the wine.

"Queen I been wanting to kiss your kips since the first time I saw you so I'm asking you can I please see how soft they are." Nelly said.

"Yes," I said blushing.

He got up and leaned over me and kissed my kips. He pulled back and said, "You so sexy."

"Let's go," I said grabbing his hand.

I led Nelly up the back way to my old room. I couldn't wait to get to the room. As soon as we shut the door our clothes were off in seconds. His dick was standing. I was so hot and wet. It had been so long since I had some dick. He peeled off my thong and push me onto the bed. He dropped down to his knees and started eating my love box. I rubbed his waves as he sucked on my clit. He had me at my peek.

My moans started getting louder but before I could cum he hopped up and got between my legs.

"Put a rubber on," I said stopping him. He put one on fast and jumped right back between my legs. He slid the head of his dick in my pussy.

"Ahh...Nelly," I sighed as he hit my g-spot. He was hitting the spot so hard that I dug my nails deep down into his back.

"OH...Oh!" I screamed in satisfaction. I had two orgasms back to back.

"Ah shit...This pussy is tight," he uttered as he shot a nut into the rubber. He pulled out and laid next to me. A few minutes later he was back inside my guts again. We fucked and laid with each other all night long.

I was up bright and early the next morning getting ready to head back to Indianapolis.

"Am I going to see you again?" Nelly asked.

"I will be back soon," I said.

"Well be careful and hit me if you need me. I'm still a hood nigga at heart," Nelly said.

I said my goodbyes to Kenya, cousin Pooder and cousin Punkin.

Me and Tiffany waved our hands as we headed inside the airport.

Chapter 33

Sade and Porsche was outside waiting on me when I walked out the airport.

"Family this is my other sister Tiffany. She helped me out when I first moved to Miami years ago and she just helped us all out again. She's official," I said as we climbed inside the Bentley.

"Hey girl. I'm Porsche and this is out sister Sade. It's going to take her a minute to like you," Porsche said.

When we turned down the block it was mad people out like always. Kids were riding bikes having fun and the grown ups were out smoking and drinking. Porsche pulled up in front of the house and we all jumped out. I hoped out fresh to death as usual. The first face I see was Dukes. He had gotten tall.

"Damn how did everyone know you were out but me," he said walking up to me.

"I had to bust a move fast but I'm back," I said.

"What you got going on," he asked me.

"Putting it together and you."

"I'm just out here chilling enjoying the fun. I see you doing big things with that Bentley. Niggas been out here for years and they still ain't rode in one of those. That's that old money," Duke said.

"You know me. I come from old money," I said pulling out a bank roll I left with. It was some old twenties.

"Kids come get y'all some money," I said passing the bills out.

"I'm trying to get down with you," Duke said knowing that I had a plan to get some money.

"Listen I'm not even going to lie to you. There's no way you getting money with me anymore. Me and my (Bad, Bitches, Getting, Money) click is all I need," I said meaning every word.

Before Duke could respond Money walked up on us.

"Damn, Queen you can't say what's up to a nigga?" he said.

"Man, you can kick rocks too. You know what it is with me."

"What did I do to you?" he asked as Marilyn walked up on us.

"Hey niece," Marilyn said.

I stood there and laughed at both of them standing before me like they didn't do shit.

"You going to stay mad at me forever. We family. What we not crew anymore," she asked me.

"BBGM is my crew. All you people out here are fake as hell and can kiss my ass," I said pointing at everyone. I looked down and saw Marilyn ball her fist up. I would never forget what she did to me. She didn't know how it felt to be caged in a room.

"Why are you so mad?" asked Money.

"I'm mad because this bitch."

She hit me before I could finish my sentence. She tried to throw another one but I got on her ass hitting her all in the face. I stepped back to let her get right because I dreamed of the day I would kick her ass. We were in the street going at it like two pit bulls. I got to beating her ass out there. She couldn't do anything with me.

"Somebody help that girl," someone yelled.

With every punch I told her why I was doing it. Someone yanked me off her and I spun around ready to fight with them also.

"Damn Baby girl you ready to fight me too," Big Jesus said. I stood there listening to my heart pound in my chest ready to get back at Marilyn ass. Marilyn got up off the ground with blood all over her. She went to her car and came back with a .380 in her hand.

"What you going to do shoot me because you know you can't fuck with these hands or is it because you a snake? My dad always told me if you pull a gun you better use it so what you going to do?" I asked not scared.

"Put that gun down. Y'all are tripping out here. We family," Big Jesus said standing in front of Marilyn and her gun,

"She use to be my ave but that's long and gone," I said walking up to my house.

Once inside the house we all sat down.

"I want to say it's time to get this money. This the plans. I have four bricks of raw and twenty pounds of K-2 coming. I already paid for the shit so we have to get to the money without taking loss. Now we going to take the four and make six the way I'm able to get the $160,000 I spent back. Every flip we should be able to put up money, put up our reup and do whatever else we need to do. I choose to bring us all together because you three have shown me all the love in the world. Tiffany dad went $35,000 for each brick and for the twenty pounds he want $10,000 plus $10,000 to bring it to the city. Sade you can continue to work your job and move the smoke, and you two open the spots, collect the money and make sure Sade get it," I said.

****

Our talk was interrupted by my phone ringing.

"Hello." I said picking it up.

"Queen, this Kym. I need to speak with you about something important," she said.

"Come over I'm at the house."

Five minutes later there was a knock at the front door. I peeked out the blinds to make sure she wasn't trying to set me up for the kill.

"What up Kym?" I asked as I opened the door.

"I need to speak with you alone," Kym said.

"We about to go into the room and holler in private so let me know if y'all need me," I said to the girls as I led Kym down the hall.

"Queen, I know you look at me different because before you left I was bad but your grandpa got me and your mother on this shit. He even dated that chick Amber that got you at your party years ago but this about your dad," she said.

"What about him?" I asked.

"Cash didn't kill him."

"Who did then?" I asked not feeling this talk.

"It all was your grandpa."

I believed her because I remember Black Jesus saying something in his letter but I wasn't going to let her know I did.

"How you know all this?" I asked.

"They sent me on a run and thought I was out of the house but I wasn't so I heard your grandpa planning it. He was mad at your daddy because he was the man now and didn't want your grandpa to get his hands dirty. He was saying Black Jesus looked at him like an old wash up dude. Then two days after that Black Jesus was killed," she said crying.

"Why are you now telling me this shit?" I asked.

"I always wanted to tell you but I didn't believe you could think back then but you older now and can stand on your own. Remember a woman can think is dangerous," she said.

"Okay listen as soon as y'all in the house alone I need you to flock that porch light for me. I know Marilyn is going out to a party." I said leading her to the front door.

"Porsche let me get a few grams so I can give to Kym," I said.

Chapter 34

Tiffany you going to have to stay in a room or go over to your moms house just in case my auntie want to come back.

After dropping Tiffany off me and Porsche sat in the living room talking. I broke down everything Kym said to me. It was 1:30a.m. when Kym flicked the light twice. Dressed in all black we both pulled our hoody over our heads, checked our guns and rushed across the street. The block was dead. Kym waved us toward the back.

"Where is he?" I whispered.

"He's in the bed sleeping," Kym said.

"Nobody else is here?" I asked handing Kym a stack of money.

"No everybody went out for the night,"

We crept down the hall towards Big Jesus office where he do most of his sleeping. I saw that he was laid back in his love seat with his mouth wide open. We stepped into the office and we both just looked at the snake before us. I kicked his leg.

"What the fuck?" he yelled about to hop up until Porsche cold steel met his head.

"Queen?" Big Jesus said. "What's going on with her pointing a gun at my head. Y'all need to get y'all little asses out of my house before it be a problem," Big Jesus said.

"Bitch ass snake. I know about all the snake shit you been on. You killed your own son for the streets then send me to jail," I said slapping him with my gun.

He put his head down like the bitch he was,

"Remember what goes around comes around. Now it's time for you to meet your maker," I said letting two shots go into his head.

Porsche put his gun away and grabbed her knife. She chopped off his right hand. We headed back the way we came. Kym was at the table nodding off the dope. I let off a shot in the back of Kym's head. I turned up the oven, poured gas all over the house and lot the curtains on fire. The streets was going to talk about this after they found Big Jesus' body without a right hand.

"R.I.P daddy," I said looking up to the dark sky as we headed back to my crib.

****

Porsche was looking for something to stick Big Jesus' hand on. When she found it she jumped in her car and smash off. Ten minutes later she pulled up to the curb.

"Where you go?" I asked.

"I went to the park on Udell and put that stick in the ground with a note that said. "Never should you bite the hand that feed your family but I wore gloves," she said smiling.

By this time police was everywhere on the block. People turned coming out of they houses. Me and Porsche sat on the car eating chips watching the show.

"Girl that's your granddad house," some old woman said.

"So what you want me to do?" I asked looking at her.

"No…No…No…," Marilyn pulled up with Money on her heels.

She turned and looked at me, "Why aren't you doing anything?" she asked.

"For the second time, what do y'all want me to do. He bit the hand that feed him," I said laughing.

Chapter 35

One Month Later…

"Queen, get down!" yelled Porsche pushing me between two cards.

Boom! Boom! Boom! Boom! Boom! Boom! six shots lit up the parking lot of Family Dollar on Martin Luther King as we came out of the store. I was ducking low. Boom! Boom! Boom! three more shots came our way busting out the front window of the store and knocking out the car window also. The shots rocked the car back and forth.

Boom! Boom! Boom! shots filled the car. Whoever it was shooting at us knew we were ducking behind the car and they were using everything they had.

"On the count of three we get up and handle this because I'm not going to sit here and just get killed. One, two, three," I said.

We hopped up guns blasting Boom! Boom! Boom! Boom! Boom! Boom! Boom! We let of shots, while running up the block getting away. Whoever was shooting peeled out the parking lot.

"Come on lets het the car," Porsche said running off towards the car.

Porsche yelled pulling the car next to me, "Come on, bitch get in!"

We hit 28th Street heading towards the crib.

"You good bitch?" You ain't get hit did you?" Porsche asked, looking over at me.

"Bitch I'm Queen Bee. Bees don't bleed we just sting and make honey," I said laughing. I was high and a little tipsy off the coolers we had drunk before.

Whoever shot at us was trying to kill us. I didn't know who was shooting but figured it was either people who wasn't getting any more money out there since I spread my wings or Marilyn bitch ass calling the shots in the shadows. I didn't know but was sure to find out sooner or later.

"We can't be slipping like that again. We almost got touched. I'm glad I was looking around," Porsche said, as we pulled in front of the crib.

I knew Porsche was speaking the truth but my ego was too big for it so I let it talk.

"Fuck everybody. It's us against them. If they asking for a war, than all they had to do was say that shit. Bitch, we BBGM, who's gon' touch us, huh?," I asked while looking at Porsche.

"Nobody but listen to me. You remember you told me about that one time them bitches tried to jump y'all at the mall and Black Jesus told y'all don't try to fight the world at least with physical force. There's other ways to win, other ways to get what you want. The mind is the greatest weapon, not our fist, not our gun, not our money, not our soldiers, but our minds. That shit stuck with me so we have to move smart," Porsche said hopping out the car.

"Bitch y'all need to get to the house. Somebody just shot at us coming out of Family Dollar," Porsche yelled into the phone.

"Who was that?" I asked laying on the sofa.

"Sade and Tiff. They on they way. We all need to stay together until we all can figure out who's doing all this shooting," Porsche said.

"That's right killa," I said.

"Bitch, this shit is real. Somebody just tried to take our heads off and you laying here playing like shit is good. Until we figure this shit out you need to stay low and I need you to get back on point. You been slipping a lot fucking with them coolers. You be over doing it bitch," Porsche said.

"Ok sister," I said.

****

Our crew was click tight and I became to love Tiff like a sister. She was out of the hotel and staying with me at the crib, while Kenya was still staying in Miami with cousin Punkin. But over all the crew was all close together, which consisted of only four of us. It was me, Porsche, Sade and Tiff. Together we had the whole city in a chokehold. In the few months that we had put BBGM together, we were now copping big every week. Everybody played their role good. There wasn't any hate because we all getting money.

We all had went to the car lot where I got my Bentley and they copped something good.

Sade had a Maserati, Tiff had an Aston Martin truck and you know Porsche had to get her Porsche 911. Then after that I hand custom gold and diamond encrusted BBGM inside a stack of money. Everywhere we went we shut it down. No female crew in the city was making noise like us. We were shutting down nigga's and bitches spots and I think that's why people were shooting at us. When we stepped out to a club or somewhere everyone knew who we were. We wasn't giving niggas the time of day.

****

"Queen get the fuck up bitch," Sade said throwing a pillow at me.

I opened my eyes to Sade, Tiff and Porsche sitting with food on the table.

"What's up bitch?" I said sitting up.

"You okay"? She asked.

143

"Yeah I'm okay. You know when I go out it's going to be on my time. Whoever it was shooting wasn't about that life. They want the top spot but don't know how to take it from us," I said.

"We gon' find whoever it is and put this shit to rest asap," Porsche said.

"But until we find out whoever it is we all need to stay low and Queen you need to stop drinking them coolers like water. We have to stay on point," Tiff said.

"Okay, I'm a fall back on the coolers and stay low but if y'all don't hurry up I'm going back to what I do and that's spreading my honey and shining on the city," I said

Everybody started laughing and eating. Right here it was my family and we were going to turn up the heat.

****

"What the fuck you mean you wasn't able to get at her?" Oh you missed her because she was ducking? What the fuck were you doing shooting in the air? I knew yo' bitch ass was the wrong person to send for this job. She's trying to take my spot and she's one of my enemies and you taking this shit as it it's a game. You might as well get a head start and get the hell out of the city because if I or any of my people see you, you are dead." Click.

Chapter 36

Today was the Christmas party of the year. I been in the house for the past month like I promised the girls. I was so bored staying in the house while the girls was out in the city handling all the business and trying to figure out who was at our head.

Porsche, Tiff, Sade and I were downtown in Chicago getting some clothes at Neimans and Saks for the Christmas party at Club 9-1 Butterfly on 71st St in Indianapolis. Everybody who was anybody was gonna be in that spot. The chick who was throwing the party father was some bigtime kingpin back in the day so she knew some important people. Me and the girls was determined to shut the building down.

"Hello ladies, what can I do for you today," one of the sale reps asked stepping from behind the counter at this shoe store.

"I have this red sheath dress and need some footwear to go with it," I said looking at some cute neon leather sandals.

"I just got a new pair of Christian Louboutin heels in just morning. They should go great with your dress. They red and open toes. And what can I do for the other ladies," the sale rep asked going to help the girls out.

The sale rep laced all us with heels and another dress. We all stepped out the mall and hopped into Sade car so we could get back to the city. It was still early so we had time. Sade was dropping everybody off to where they were going and we were going to meet back up at my crib later.

****

It was re-up time so I had to go home and count out $975,000 for the bricks and $40,000 for the synthetic weed which equal out to $1,015,000. My job was to make sure all the money was right for the shipment. I made sure all windows and doors were locked and went to my dad old safe. That's where I kept the majority of the money. I had a few different spots around the city too. I grab three duffle bags that the girls have given to me. I dragged the bags into the living room, got the money counter and rubber bands.

It took me two in half hours to count out the money for the shipment and another hour to count the rest. The crew would split the remainder of the money left.

****

After cleaning the house up and grabbing something to eat I fall asleep on the sofa. The sound of my phone going off woke me up. I looked at the phone.

"Damn," I said. I had been sleep for too long. It was a little past 10:30 p.m. I had already showered so I ran into my room to get dressed.

"Come on bitch. I'm trying to party!" Porsche shouted coming into my room.

"I'm coming," I said, putting on my heels. I stood up and checked myself one last time.

"Let's go turn the heat up," I said stepping out the house behind Porsche.

When we all pulled up back-to-back at the 9-1 Butterfly each of us hopped out and gave the keys to the valet. It was going on 11:20 so we rushed inside. People were still waiting outside in the cold waiting to get it.

"Who are them bitches?"

"That's the BBGM," I heard some chick say, as we stepped through the doors.

146

"BBGM, I see y'all looking good," The DJ shouted over the music as we stepped into the main room. Porsche knew the DJ and had him make the shout out. But everybody in the building acknowledged our presence and raised a drink.

"I 'ma hit the bar," I said to the girls before rushing off.

"Can I please get any cooler you have back there," I told the barmaid.

I turned and scanned all the fine brothers up in the building. I locked eyes with this brother that stood about 6'2" with nice arms.

"Here you go," the barmaid said.

When I turned back around the brother caught me off guard. He was standing in front of me rocking a Stoffa sweater, Ralph Lauren pants and Edward Green shoes, Cartier glasses and a watch. I knew my clothes.

"You know when the DJ shouted BBGM out I had to see who y'all were and I didn't believe my eyes when I saw you looking all fine. I said this can't be the same chick that was standing outside the mall when she first got home from prison."

"Damn, you look different. I didn't even know that was you. What's your name again," I asked.

"SK. Yeah, I had to get myself together. I been working doing the security shit but I see you flying high."

"I been doing good but what else you been up to since getting home," I asked.

"Well I'm in school studying construction."

"That's good. Come let's dance," I said grabbing his hand leading to the floor. I had all this ass on that nigga. I had to grab his hand to make him feel this ass.

I know he was being respectful but fuck all that tonight. I was out to have fun.

"I see ya girl," Tiff said. She had some tall chocolate brother.

The DJ put on some slow music so I was standing there facing SK moving my hips. We stood there slow moving like we were the only ones in the club.

"What's on your mind," SK asked while looking down into my eyes.

"Everything from my parents to my life. Right here dancing with you just feel so right. A lot of things had went wrong in my life but not at this moment," I said.

Me and the girls flicked it up. I paid the dude to bring my own back drop of the city and it said "We run the city." We took so many pictures spreading money all over the floor. We was fly with our mini minks. Everybody was just joining into the pictures which we didn't care.

"I'm done," I said handing the photographer $1,000. When I stepped away my phone started popping. I looked at it and saw that we were all over social media. I laughed because we were shutting down social media.

The club was still going but I was tired of wearing these damn heels. I asked SK to fuck with me for the night which he said ok. I told the girls I was going home but they didn't care because they were in the V.I.P. having a ball.

****

"Yeah, bitch I been waiting for you to get home."

"Come on," I said climbing out the car.

SK helped me walk in the snow. As I fiddle with my house keys I heard something on the side of the house but it was dark. Not paying it any mind I unlocked the door let SK step in and before I could step in Boom! Boom! Boom! The last thing I remembered was a figure shooting at me. I didn't know where SK was until he came from around the door letting his gun go off.

"Shit," I heard the figure say running.

"Damn it, Queen."

My entire body went numb. Damn they for me, I thought to myself before passing out.

Chapter 37

Porsche, Sade and Tiff was driving back-to-back like mad women swerving from lane to lane down Michigan Road to get back to the hood.

"Shit, shit, shit," Porsche said with all types of murder thoughts going through her head. She was going to turn up the heat on the whole city because somebody know something. Until they find out the flower store was about to have a lot of business.

Porsche cross over 38th St to Martin Luther King and rode down the street doing 60mph. She spotted Mercedes, Tall Pussy and April coming out Marathon gas station on West 29th. She turned into the station.

"What's up Porsche?" Mercedes asked as Sade and Tiff pulled in behind Porsche's car on the side of the building. Without answering Mercedes, Porsche just pulled her 9mm out and le it answer for her.

Boom! Boom! Boom! She put three slugs into Mercedes dropping her body. Without thinking twice Sade hit Tall Pussy with one to the forehead. When they both turned around Tiff held her hand with shaking hands.

"What you waiting for. Put that work in," Porsche said.

Boom! Boom! Boom! Tiff let off three rounds with her eyes closed.

They hopped back into their cars and smashed off like that was a part of everyday life. When they pulled in front of Porsche house they all ran into the house but once they were inside Porsche slapped fire out of Tiff.

"Don't ever second guess yourself again. That bitch could have got up on you. You see us putting in work. Shit about to get ugly so we need to know if you down for this war because it's on. Our sister needs us so now isn't the time to be scared now let's get strapped," Porsche said.

"I'm down," Tiff said following Porsche into the kitchen where she hit a button on the oven and the counter opened up with all type of guns inside.

"Where all this shit come from. You got enough shit in here to tear up the whole city," Tiff said.

"Here put these on," Porsche said handing Sade and Tiff bulletproof vests. Pick what y'all want and let's go."

After a few minutes of them getting themselves together they were back out the house. They left their cars in front and hopped inside their trap car which was a 2008 Chevrolet Cargo van. Tiff took control of the wheel.

"Pull over that nigga right there, that's the nigga Dro. He used to be part of Queen's dad crew until her grandfather flipped them on him. I know his bitch ass knows something. He keeps his ears to the streets. If he don't know then so be it," Porsche said.

Porsche watched Dro go inside Vick's Liquor store and exited with a brown paper bag. He was walking towards his Cadillac. Before he could reach the door handle Porsche was out of the van letting her 9mm bark.

Boom! Boom! Boom! Boom! Porsche caught Dro all four times in the chest before he hit the ground.

Crush hopped out of Dro's car busting towards Porsche but he didn't see Sade two cars behind him.

Boom! Boom! Boom! Boom! Boom! Boom! Sade aired Crush ass out.

"Let's bounce," Sade said as they jumped in the van and Tiff pulled off.

****

"After coming home on West 28th after a Christmas part, this woman here, Queen Jesus was gunned down by someone who was waiting for her outside of her house. She's listed in critical condition. Police say they have no one in custody at this time and have no leads at this time. Again, Queen Jesus, known to the authorities as a major drug trafficker and one of the head women of BBGMM was gunned down."

"Now we going live in front of Vick's Liquor Store where two men was gunned down after leaving the liquor store. The two men were known kingpins and us to work for Black Jesus who was killed years ago. The police are only identifying the two men by nicknames at this moment. One name is Dro and other Crush when we get more information we will address it."

"I can't believe this bitch refuse to die. It's like she has 9 lives and who the fuck killed Dro and Crush. Please turn the T.V. off."

Chapter 38

Queen woke to find herself in totally unfamiliar environment. Her eyes were filled with days worth of sleep and her retinas were slow to adjust because of the lack of use, and as a result were slow to bring things into focus. She didn't know where she was all she knew was her surroundings was white and pristine. The different colors from the many monitors and machines interrupted her monotonous. Her throat was sore and parched, and her entire body ached like she had been slapped by a truck. Queen could feel the sharp stinging pain in her chest where the bullet struck, and this brought about some clarity of mind. She now remembered that she had been shot after the party.

The memory of that night slowly flashed through her mind. It came like it was a movie but she actually lived it. But how she got from her house to this bed was beyond her. She knew little, except that she been shot and now was lying in a hospital bed.

"Hey, sexy," a voice said softly from the corner of the room.

Queen turned her head in the direction from which it came. SK was seated by her bedside doing his college work.

"Glad you decided to wake and join us," SK continued. He took her hand and kissed it.

Queen swallowed but it came with great difficulty. She had an IV hooked up to my arm providing me with the vital sustaining fluids that I needed, but still I had not swallowed, spoken, or even opened by mouth in days. Talking came hard. I had many questions that I needed answered asap.

SK poured water in a small cup and lifted it to my lips allowing me to take small sips and it felt so good.

"I'm glad to see you're awake now, Mrs. Jesus. You've lost a good amount of blood, but you will be ok just as long as you get some rest and heal up," the doctor said.

"How long have I been here?" I asked.

"A week."

"Damn a week?" I said to myself.

"Yeah a week and if it wasn't for this young man been there with you maybe you would have dead. This young man saved your life," the doctor said smiling at us.

I looked into SK eyes and said, "Thank you. You've been here with me this whole week?" I asked SK.

"Every day. I called my school and job and let them know I needed two weeks off to help my woman since she been shot," SK said.

"Make sure she get some rest," the doctor said leaving the two of us in the room.

"You feeling ok?" asked SK wiping my face.

"I feel like shit," I said.

"You'll get better. I'm here for you until it's time for you to be released."

"I don't remember anything," I said.

"All I know is as soon as you opened the door I stepped inside and someone came from the side of the house shooting so I grabbed my strap and let it go. I called the police and went through your phone and text your sister."

My mind was everywhere because the last thing I remember was pulling up to the house.

"Damn someone's trying to kill me," I said.

"Yeah and if I wasn't with you they would have because whoever it was, was waiting so whoever it is knows you," SK said.

SK was right about that, I thought.

"I think you should get a new crib because it's not safe to be in that house. You getting too much money to be staying in the hood still," SK said.

"Hell nah. Black Jesus been in that house for years and since he left it to me I was staying there. He didn't raise me to run from a problem," I said.

I was about to speak again but stopped when the door opened with two guys walking in with gold badges hanging from their necks.

"Mrs. Jesus, you know who tried to kill you?" Detective Hernandez asked.

"If I told you then that means you would be getting a free check but let me know when you find the nigga or bitch," I said looking him in the eyes.

"You think this is a game. Someone want you dead. We know about somebody trying you at the Family Dollar? His partner said.

"Can you please listen, I don't know anything about what you guys are saying. Tell your C.I. to give you some better information but until I'm around my lawyer don't come back," I said.

"Well ok then fucker. The next time don't call my boys," Detective Deer said as they headed for the door.

"I want bitches. I will keep it in the streets," I yelled as they slammed the door.

Chapter 39

Porsche and Sade sat in the booth at Olive Garden eating and talking. Out of no where some short dude with a hat and sunglasses sat down at the table.

"Who the fuck are you," Sade said.

"That's Sugar Foot," Porsche said still eating.

"What's good, Sugar Foot? What's on your mind?" Porsche asked.

Sugar Foot looked around as sweat started dripping down his face. He was looking everywhere besides Porsche's eyes.

"What's good with you, Sugar Foot. You coming in here fucking up me and my sister meal sweating and not looking at me like something is wrong."

"Yeah, you right my bad but it's about Marilyn and Money."

"Fuck Marilyn, she's not to be trusted. Whatever you have going on with her keep it between y'all because I don't rock with snakes," Porsche said.

"Naw it's just she been on a lot of back shit. She trying to have someone kill me. I been laying low for a while now and figure I can come to you for a little help."

"What makes you think that I would help you and what did you do to the bitch?" Porsche asked.

Porsche knew that type of nigga Sugar Foot was. He would turn on his own mother for the right price. He was a nigga that came from Texas a few years back because he stole some bricks from a Kingpin down there.

"Marilyn want to kill me because she paid me to do something that I really couldn't do but the greed got the best of me when I seen the $50,000 on the table so I took it without thinking."

"So what did the bitch want you to do?"

"This is crazy. I got love for you and Queen. Y'all like my sisters. Even though y'all split up. I'm telling you all this because I know y'all some stand up females."

"Fuck all that get to the point," Porsche said taking a bite of her food.

"Marilyn is the one that keep sending people to off Queen. I know it's hard for you to believe since they family and all y'all grow up together but this is real. She gave me the money and told me to get the job done. I could have got Queen when y'all came out of Family Dollar but I kept missing because I really didn't want to kill y'all. Since I kept missing now she's trying to get at me. I offered to give her the $50,000 back but she told me to give it to my mom to bury me. She even think Queen killed her dad and Kim. I think she's really shitty y'all sling that shit like Patti Labelle did them pres. I really need y'all help on this because I don't trust anybody," Sugar Foot said.

"This isn't a set up is it?" Porsche asked,

"Porsche I wont play like this when you can easy kill me right now. Marilyn said y'all know something that she don't want to get out plus y'all have took all the spots in the hood. She still have a few people that's loyal to her on the getting money tip but overall y'all have the city on lock. She trying to get at y'all whole crew."

"So what are you asking me to do for you?" asked Porsche looking at Sade and Sugar Foot.

"I need to get out of my bm house because she talk too much and it would be a matter of time before she tell someone that I'm there. I just need to lay low for a while until we can figure things out then y'all can put me to work."

"This what I 'ma do for you. I'm gonna let you stay in a crib we have out this way until we handle this. It's food and anything else you need already there. Don't come out once you in that house and don't open the door unless it's me or Sade," Porsche said.

"Let's go drop this nigga off at the spot so we can get down to business," Porsche said.

****

"Sade where you been? I haven't seen you in a long time. You and your little brother are hell," Sugar Foot said.

"I been chilling doing me. I was around," Sade said.

Sade pulled into the driveway of the spot. This was going to be one of their spots but they been doing a lot of dirt there.

"Come on," Porsche said getting out as Sade killed the engine.

Sade and Porsche led Sugar Foot through the back door of the house.

"Damn this spot is nice. Who else going to be here with me?" Sugar Foot asked admiring all the new things in the house. Everything had plastic over it.

While Sugar Foot walked around the house he never noticed Sade walking behind him. When they got to the bathroom she fired two shots in the back of the head and pushed him into the tub.

Chapter 40

"Damn bitches, I started to feel like I didn't have any sisters anymore," I said, as Sade, Tiff and Porsche entered the hospital room.

"Bitch please. You know we won't just leave you like that but we happy you coming home today," Tiff said giving me a hug,

"Yeah hoe," Sade said.

"I 'ma let y'all have some time. I'm gonna step out and grab a pop, Queen." SK said walking out the room.

"Damn that's the fine brother that was at the club. He been keeping us updated," Tiff said.

"Yeah, he rolled with me back to the crib that night I got shot. If he wasn't with me, I would have died."

"Is he good?" asked Tiff.

"He's one hundred. Good dude. If he wouldn't called the police for me I wouldn't be here so he was my blessing."

"What's up, Porsche you ain't gone give your sister no hug?" I asked.

Porsche was standing off to the side texting on her phone. I knew she felt some type of way for letting me go home by myself.

"Hey sis, I'm just a little fucked up right now because I been fighting with myself every since you been in here when I knew someone was out there trying to get at us," Porsche said.

"I'm good, sis. I'm still standing. They didn't do shit but make me shitty."

"Yeah, I know." Porsche said smiling.

"Why is this the first time y'all pulled up on me?"

"We had to go hunting first to let the streets know we weren't playing and still standing and we not to be fucked with. And do you know how hard it would have been to see you laid up in here all fucked up so we just stayed away. We knew you were good," Porsche said.

"Okay that's what's up?" "I seen on my phone that Dro, Crush, Mercedes, Tall Pussy and April all got killed in one night," I said.

"Yeah all that shit happened after you got hit but this is going to fuck your head up but I have to tell you. That bitch Marilyn been the one sending ones at us. She even think you had something to do with Big Jesus and Kim," Porsche said.

Damn that did fuck my head up. I knew we weren't tight anymore but for her to be sending people at me she must be taking this shit to the heart. We could have handled this a different way.

"I know your brain is rocking with question because mines was but it's one hundred and the nigga Sugar Foot gave me and Sade the details. It was said we knew something about Marilyn that she didn't want to get out too," Porsche said.

"You believe that greed ass nigga?" I asked.

"Hell yeah I believe him. It all add up. We ain't beefing with anyone because we letting everyone in the city eat. That bitch mad we put her out of business and she don't want you to put that statement out," Porsche said.

I never sat and added up the facts because I was busy doing me. I should have knew the deal coming from the streets but I never told anyone else about Marilyn statement but I guess she's trying to get me before I do then me taking over the city really didn't help either. I just might post it on the internet.

"I want to talk to Sugar Foot," I said.

"R.I.P.," Sade said smiling.

It was a knock at the door then the nurse came in. She had my papers in her hand so I could sign out.

"You better take care of yourself and heal up. Also make sure you do some type of workout on your body," the nurse said.

"Thanks for being here for my sister," Tiff said to SK as he walked back in the room.

"Yeah sis, he's someone you should keep around more," Sade said smiling.

"I think I might do that sisters," I said.

****

We all were inside my house billing, talking and laughing.

"I'm about to go in here and cook us something to eat," SK said walking into the kitchen.

"Damn Tiff roll up some of that good shit so I can get my head right. I haven't smoked in weeks," I said.

"Sis, why don't you stay at my crib for a while so I can get you back in shape," Sade said.

"Yeah that would be getting in shape and you would be safe," Porsche said.

"I see what y'all trying to do and I'm not going for it. This is my hood and my house so I'm not going anywhere. I'm going to kill whoever this bitch send my way and sooner then later. She will show her face and when she do I would be there. This shit then got deep and personal for me since she want to send people to my dad house," I said.

"You a hard headed bitch but it's coo I already knew you wasn't going to go to my spot," Sade said.

SK walked into the living room with two pizzas in his hand.

"That shit looks good as hell," Porsche hungry ass said.

"Yeah, I use to make these in prison all the time. I'm cold with this cooking shit and y'all will," SK said.

Chapter 41

Me and SK was up and out the house early. I had to make a few moves and I was going to drop SK off at work. SK has moved into the house with me and Tiff. He said it was only until I handled whatever I needed to handle but who was kidding, he knew he was there to stay. We had fun together.

We jumped in my Bentley and peeled off speeding until we got to Martin Luther King. I had a good plan to smoke this bitch Marilyn out. We had the same family so I couldn't go around killing them but I knew my plan was going to work. I popped in Cardi B, and turned it up to the max.

"Be Careful" was playing as I got my thoughts together because I was about to turn the heat up on this bitch and she didn't even know it. She had missed too many times.

First of business was getting the target off my back and that was jumping into another car. Being in the Bentley had put me in the spotlight because everyone in the city knew my car from me stunting on them so I pulled into the car dealership where I bought it. I was going to cop me something new and just put the Bentley up for a while. I saw this Porsche Cayenne Turbo GT Coupe.

"That's a sexy bitch right there," I said to SK getting out the car.

"Hi you doing?" The same dealer asked me with a smile on his face.

"Trying to keep my head above water, how about ya'self?" I asked.

"Hustling like always. I see you looking at the coupe. She just came in a few weeks ago."

"Yeah," I said still looking at the car.

"So what you trying to do today?" He asked.

"I'm trying to cash out on it today so how much we talking about," I asked patting my handbag.

"Give me $100,000 and she's your?"

"Damn how I buy a Bentley lesser," I asked.

"See the Bentley was years old but her, she's a new body and came out two years ago."

"It's cool let's get it cracking," I said.

The salesman had my paperwork done less then twenty minutes and I pulled off the lot with SK following me to the storage unit to put up the Bentley.

SK jumped in the car with me after parking the Bentley so I could drop him off to work.

"Hello?"

"What's up, girl," Tiff said, answering the phone.

"Where Sade and Porsche at?" I asked.

"They right here chilling watching me roll up," Tiff said.

"Well meet me at Olive Gardens on West 38th because I have something to talk to y'all about that's important. Breakfast on me," I said hanging up.

"Who was you talking to?" asked Sade.

"Queen. She said meet her at Olive Garden on 38th because she has something to talk to us about and breakfast on her," Tiff said.

"Come on. Let's go," Sade said, grabbing her keys off the table. They all piled into Sade's Maserati and headed to Olive Garden.

Sade pulled into the parking lot. It wasn't that many cars. They all was looking for Queen's Bentley but she wasn't no where in sight.

"This bitch had us drive out here and she's not here yet?" Sade said Parking.

Sade whipped her phone out and called Queen.

"Bitch, I see y'all just hop out the car," Queen said hanging up and getting out her car.

"Damn bitch," Tiff said, looking around my new car. "I see how you feel? Bitches at our heads and you stunting on them with a Coupe. I gotta get my shit together," Tiff said admiring the ride.

"Why the hell you call us out here just to talk. What's up bitch, you good?" Porsche asked.

We walked into Olive Garden got seated and got some food. I began talking after out food touched the table.

"Yeah, I'm good to answer your question. The reason I asked y'all to meet me out here because I wanted to holler at y'all. It's time to turn up the heat on Marilyn. I put my Bentley in the storage because everyone in the city knows my ride and that alone makes me a target feel me. I need y'all to put up y'all shit too and grab something else because the city knows y'all shit too. I told the dealer y'all might be pulling up on him so he's waiting," I said.

"What you got on your mind though," Sade asked.

"Okay, since me and Marilyn has the same family I can't touch them so we going to get at Money's peoples so he will come out of hiding with her. I know his sister running the candy store on Paris, his mother's house is right on Indianapolis and his brother has a weed spot on Highland. I was thinking about having SK sit on the brother while we get at his mother and sister because after this the bodies is going to be dropping. Make sure y'all keep them hammers on y'all even when you sitting. And Tiff change your routine because everyone knows you in live with the mall," I said looking at her.

"It's about time we get our hands dirty," Sade said.

"We BBGM," I said.

"BBGM!" We all said.

"Look, I 'ma get at y'all later on," I said leaving.

SK text and said we will meet me at the house. He had his partner take him home to get his car. I knew I had been gone all morning and miss my man. I didn't even get to get me any morning dick so I was about to go home and fuck his lights out. I turned down 28th and could see SK Benz parked in front of the house. It was a black Camaro sitting there too but I didn't know whose car it was so I kept pushing down the block. I parked on 27th and just walked through the alley so I could go through the back way.

When I got to the back door my stomach started flipping so I knew something wasn't right and Black Jesus always told me to listen to my stomach. I pulled my 9mm out, then opened the door. I crept through the dark house low to the ground. Laying in a puddle of bleed was a body, thinking it was SK I went to look and as I bent down a shot rung out passed my head. Turning to look where it came from I heard foot steps coming towards me so I let off two shots.

Boom! Boom!

The front door opened and someone bolted out the house. I ran to the front door in pursuit of whomever it was in my house. The Camaro peeled off down the block. I ran out in the street and began firing.

Boom! Boom! Boom! Boom! the back window busted.

I ran back inside the crib and flicked on the lights. There were two bodies on the floor. I shut the door and went over to take a look at the two dudes. One of the dudes I knew to be Money's cousin and the other I didn't know. I went from room to room looking for SK. He was laying on the floor tied up with blood coming out his thigh. I rush over to him and untied him.

"SK," I said hugging him. I started crying.

"It's good baby, it's good," he told me.

"It's not good. Someone trying to kill me and damn near killed you today. It would have fucked me up if they while have sealed the deal. It's time to stop playing," I said.

"Baby just give me some info on these niggas and I'm going to handle this," SK said.

When I walked in the living room SK was going through the dead dudes pockets. He pulled out a cellphone and press talk calling the last number.

"Is it done?" the voice asked. I knew it had to be Marilyn's.

"Yeah," SK answered.

"Money will meet you to give you the money," she said before hanging up.

SK looked at me as I sat there not believing Marilyn was going this length to get me killed.

"Queen, I'm down for you and you should know this by now. I been staying out of your business and letting you stand on your own but today they crossed the line. I know this is your daddy's house but it's time to move. You have let the streets into your house and that's not good because this is a big problem. I'm staying here too now and them two niggas could have killed me today. I put my gun down once I got home but they have woke up the beast. Come on ride to my crib with me," SK said teeing up his thigh then walking out the door.

Chapter 42

While waiting on SK to come back out I FaceTime Porsche to update her on what happen at the house. She was over Sade's house watching the kids while she went to work.

"What the hell Queen?" Porsche said as I gave her the detail.

"Me and SK on our way back to the house. Just meet us there. I parked my car around the corner so you not going to see it," I said.

"Okay sus, baby daddy is on his way home now so I be there."

SK stayed on Georgetown Road and it would take him twenty minutes on the street to get back to the hood but he hopped on the highway and was there in five minutes.

When we walked in the house Porsche and Tiff was already in there looking at the two bodies on the floor.

"You know that's Money cousin and Duke little brother Dre," Porsche said.

"What?" I said looking at Dre.

When I went to prison Dre was a little nigga asking for money to buy candy. He had long braids and a mouth full of VV's so I didn't recognize him.

"What happen anyway?" Porsche asked shaking her head.

"Like I said I parked on 27th so I came through the back door and when I came in I saw a body on the floor thinking it was SK, I bent down to check but I felt a wind come across my face so when I looked up the nigga was coming at me so

I hit him twice then another ran out the door and peeled out in a yellow Camaro," I said.

"Yellow Camaro with black strips on it?" Porsche asked.

"Yeah."

"That's the little nigga Chevy. Let's go I know where he stay," Porsche said.

We all piled into SK Benz with Tiff driving. Me and SK sat in the back while Porsche sat up front showing Tiff where to go. SK had opened the bag he had went to get from his house and inside was different types of hand guns.

"Slow down it's the house in the middle with the flowers surrounding the porch," Porsche said but before she could finish her sentence SK was already out of the car rushing up onto the porch in seconds with his gun in hand. Me, Tiff and Porsche sat inside the car just watching every move he made since we weren't able to get out of the car ourselves and follow him to the house. Sitting there watching him really pissed me off because I didn't know what he was doing. Every move we made needed to be planned out because it was life or death.

"What the fuck is your man doing? He's on some bullshit and I hope he doesn't fuck shit up for us," Porsche said shaking her head while playing with her twin .45's.

I could tell that Tiff was scared because she kept looking around and I watched as her hand shook while they were on the steering wheel.

"Just calm down Tiff. She will be over soon," I said patting her on the shoulders. She gave me a weak smile back.

SK walked to the front door and knocked on it a few times. As he stood back the curtain in the front window moved and a lady's face popped into it. SK said something to her and whatever it was got her to open the door and step out onto the porch. The woman was all smiles as she listened to SK talk. She started touching all over SK arms and chest while she laughed. She kept looking back inside her house like she was scared someone might pop up. The whole time the two talked on the front porch SK kept his hands behind his back. He kept his gun behind his leg out of the way of the woman's eye sight.

"Who the fuck was that at the front door momma?" Chevy asked yelling throughout the house.

The woman stuck her head inside the house and yelled to Chevy, "Boy, don't worry about it. It's a friend of mines." Then she turned back toward SK.

"Friend who momma," Chevy asked opening the front door at the same time SK dumped three shells into the woman's stomach but before her body could hit the floor SK pushed it inside the house leaving her on the floor by the door. We watched SK let off shots while Chevy tried to haul ass up the front stairs.

"Girl that nigga ain't playing no games. He's the right one and I'm glad you chose him. Shid he need to hook me up with his brother or cousin," Porsche said as we watched the upstairs window opened and Chevy began walking on the roof to the side so he could climb down to get away from a shooting SK.

Porsche cocked her gun and hopped out the car. She ran across the street up to the side and as soon as Chevy's two feet touched the ground she fired two shells inside his head dropping him where he stood.

SK came running out the house at the same time Porsche did the side of the house. They piled back into the car and we rolled off like nothing happened. I was hoping no one saw us.

"So, who's next on the hit list or where are we going?" asked Tiff as we drove up 30th Street stopping at the red light.

"We have to get everyone that's not with us, that bitch Marilyn and that pussy Money has me fucked up. They have woke up the beast inside of me that I had caged but since they did it's time for me to feed him. Y'all said that Money and Duke were cousins and the little dude that came into our house were Duke brother so I feel we should hit Duke before he have time to strike us after finding out his brother is dead. I know he knew about them coming to get us," SK said reloading his gun.

"This the type of fun I'm talking about Big Bro. I like the laid back you but love the killer," Porsche said smiling.

"Shut up bitch, you just like all this damn killing," I said.

To Be Continued....

Lock Down Publications and Ca$h Presents
Assisted Publishing Packages

Due to an increase in the price of services we have increased our prices. The prices below reflect the price increase as of 11/1/24.

BASIC PACKAGE	UPGRADED PACKAGE
$699	$1000
Editing	Typing
Cover Design	Editing
Formatting	Cover Design
	Formatting
	Upload eBooks to Amazon
	Upload Paperback to Amazon
ADVANCE PACKAGE	**LDP SUPREME PACKAGE**
$1,400	$1,700
Typing	Typing
Editing (line editing/content)	Editing (line editing/content)
Cover Design	Cover Design
Formatting	Formatting
Copyright Registration	Copyright Registration
Proofreading	Proofreading
Upload eBooks to Amazon	Set up Amazon Account
Upload Paperback to Amazon	Upload eBooks to Amazon
	Upload Paperback to Amazon
	Advertise on LDP's Amazon and Facebook Page

***

Other services available upon request.
Additional charges may apply

Lock Down Publications
P.O. Box 944
Stockbridge, GA 30281-9998
Phone: 470 303-9761
Email: lockdownpublications@gmail.com

Submission Guideline

Submit the first three chapters of your completed manuscript to ldpsubmissions@gmail.com. In the subject line add **Your Book's Title**. The manuscript must be in a Word Doc file and sent as an attachment. Document should be in Times New Roman, double spaced, and in size 12 font. Also, provide your synopsis and full contact information. If sending multiple submissions, they must each be in a separate email.

Have a story but no way to send it electronically? You can still submit to LDP/Ca$h Presents. Send in the first three chapters, written or typed, of your completed manuscript to:

LDP: Submissions Dept
P.O. Box 944
Stockbridge, GA 30281-9998

DO NOT send original manuscript. Must be a duplicate. Provide your synopsis and a cover letter containing your full contact information.

Thanks for considering LDP and Ca$h Presents.

NEW RELEASES

BLOODLINE OF A SAVAGE 1-3
THESE VICIOUS STREETS 1-3
RELENTLESS GOON 1-3
BY PRINCE A. TAUHID

THE BUTTERFLY MAFIA 1-3
BY FUMIYA PAYNE

A THUG'S STREET PRINCESS 1&2
BY MEESHA

CITY OF SMOKE 3
BY MOLOTTI

GET IT IN SLUGS 1 &2
BY B. STALL

STANDING ON HER BUSINESS 1&2
BY DG SANTANA

STEPPERS 1,2&3
THE REAL BADDIES OF CHI-RAQ
BY KING RIO

THE LANE 1&2
BY KEN-KEN SPENCE

THUG OF SPADES 1&2
LOVE IN THE TRENCHES 2
CORNER BOYS
BY COREY ROBINSON

TIL DEATH 3
BY ARYANNA

THE BIRTH OF A GANGSTER 4
BY DELMONT PLAYER

PRODUCT OF THE STREETS 1-3
BY DEMOND "MONEY" ANDERSON

NO TIME FOR ERROR
BY KEESE

MONEY HUNGRY DEMONS 1-2
BY TRANAY ADAMS

HUB CITY MENACE 1-3
BY J. WHITE

A THUGGISH PASSION 1&2
LAND OF DA HOOLIGANZ 1-4
KILLAZ ON STANDBY 1&2
BY IRA B.

FO'EVA ROLLIN 1&2
BY ASSA RAYMOND BAKER

THE LEVEL UP 1&3
BY LUXURY KING

Coming Soon from Lock Down Publications/Ca$h Presents

IF YOU CROSS ME ONCE 6
ANGEL V
By Anthony Fields

A THUGS STREET PRINCESS 3
By Meesha

CORNER BOYS 2
By Corey Robinson

THA TAKEOVER
By Keith Chandler

BETRAYAL OF A G 2
By Ray Vinci

SAVAGE FAMILY EMPIRE 1&2
SOULLESS GOON 1,2&3
THE DIRTY SIDE OF MONEY 1,2&3
By Prince

FOR MY ENEMY'S SAKE
AMBITIONS OF A SLIDER
FRESH OFF DA PORCH
By IRA B.

THE TRUCKLOAD 1-4
TIPPIN' THE SCALES 1-3
BAD BITCHES WIT GUNZ 3
PROBLEM SOLVED 2
By Christopher "Diesel" Hornezes

Available Now

RESTRAINING ORDER 1 & 2
By **CA$H & Coffee**

LOVE KNOWS NO BOUNDARIES 1-3
By **Coffee**

RAISED AS A GOON I, II, III & IV
BRED BY THE SLUMS I, II, III
BLAST FOR ME I & II
ROTTEN TO THE CORE I II III
A BRONX TALE I, II, III
DUFFLE BAG CARTEL I II III IV V VI
HEARTLESS GOON I II III IV V
A SAVAGE DOPEBOY I II
DRUG LORDS I II III
CUTTHROAT MAFIA I II
KING OF THE TRENCHES
By **Ghost**

LAY IT DOWN I & II
LAST OF A DYING BREED I II
BLOOD STAINS OF A SHOTTA I & II III
By **Jamaica**

LOYAL TO THE GAME I II III
LIFE OF SIN I, II III
By **TJ & Jelissa**

IF LOVING HIM IS WRONG…I & II
LOVE ME EVEN WHEN IT HURTS I II III
By **Jelissa**

PUSH IT TO THE LIMIT
By **Bre' Hayes**

BLOODY COMMAS I & II
SKI MASK CARTEL I, II & III
KING OF NEW YORK I II, III IV V
RISE TO POWER I II III
COKE KINGS I II III IV V
BORN HEARTLESS I II III IV
KING OF THE TRAP I II
By **T.J. Edwards**

WHEN THE STREETS CLAP BACK I & II III
THE HEART OF A SAVAGE I II III IV
MONEY MAFIA I II
LOYAL TO THE SOIL I II III
By **Jibril Williams**

A DISTINGUISHED THUG STOLE MY HEART I II & III
LOVE SHOULDN'T HURT I II III IV
RENEGADE BOYS 1-4
PAID IN KARMA 1-3
SAVAGE STORMS 1-3
AN UNFORESEEN LOVE 1-3
BABY, I'M WINTERTIME COLD 1-3
A THUG'S STREET PRINCESS 1&2
By **Meesha**

A GANGSTER'S CODE 1-3
A GANGSTER'S SYN 1-3
THE SAVAGE LIFE 1-3
CHAINED TO THE STREETS 1-3
BLOOD ON THE MONEY 1-3
A GANGSTA'S PAIN 1-3
BEAUTIFUL LIES AND UGLY TRUTHS
CHURCH IN THESE STREETS
By **J-Blunt**

CUM FOR ME 1-8
An LDP Erotica Collaboration

BLOOD OF A BOSS 1-5
SHADOWS OF THE GAME
TRAP BASTARD
By **Askari**

THE STREETS BLEED MURDER 1-3
THE HEART OF A GANGSTA 1-3
By **Jerry Jackson**

WHEN A GOOD GIRL GOES BAD
By **Adrienne**

THE COST OF LOYALTY 1-3
By **Kweli**

BRIDE OF A HUSTLA 1-3
THE FETTI GIRLS 1-3
CORRUPTED BY A GANGSTA 1-4
BLINDED BY HIS LOVE
THE PRICE YOU PAY FOR LOVE 1-3
DOPE GIRL MAGIC 1-3
By **Destiny Skai**

A KINGPIN'S AMBITION
A KINGPIN'S AMBITION II
I MURDER FOR THE DOUGH
By **Ambitious**

TRUE SAVAGE 1-7
DOPE BOY MAGIC 1-3
MIDNIGHT CARTEL 1-3
CITY OF KINGZ 1&2
NIGHTMARE ON SILENT AVE
THE PLUG OF LIL MEXICO 1&2
CLASSIC CITY
By **Chris Green**

A GANGSTER'S REVENGE 1-4
THE BOSS MAN'S DAUGHTERS 1-5
A SAVAGE LOVE 1&2
BAE BELONGS TO ME 1&2
A HUSTLER'S DECEIT 1-3
WHAT BAD BITCHES DO 1-3
SOUL OF A MONSTER 1-3
KILL ZONE
A DOPE BOY'S QUEEN 1-3
TIL DEATH 1-3
IMMA DIE BOUT MINE 1-6
DYING FOR LIKES
By **Aryanna**

A DOPEBOY'S PRAYER
By **Eddie "Wolf" Lee**

THE KING CARTEL 1-3
By **Frank Gresham**

THESE NIGGAS AIN'T LOYAL 1-3
By **Nikki Tee**

GANGSTA SHYT 1-3
By **CATO**

THE ULTIMATE BETRAYAL
By **Phoenix**

BOSS'N UP 1-3
By **Royal Nicole**

I LOVE YOU TO DEATH
By **Destiny J**

I RIDE FOR MY HITTA
I STILL RIDE FOR MY HITTA
By **Misty Holt**

LOVE & CHASIN' PAPER
By **Qay Crockett**

TO DIE IN VAIN
SINS OF A HUSTLA
By **ASAD**

BROOKLYN HUSTLAZ
By **Boogsy Morina**

BROOKLYN ON LOCK 1 & 2
By **Sonovia**

GANGSTA CITY
By **Teddy Duke**

A DRUG KING AND HIS DIAMOND 1-3
A DOPEMAN'S RICHES
HER MAN, MINE'S TOO 1&2
CASH MONEY HO'S
THE WIFEY I USED TO BE 1&2
PRETTY GIRLS DO NASTY THINGS
By **Nicole Goosby**

LIPSTICK KILLAH 1-3
CRIME OF PASSION 1-3
FRIEND OR FOE 1-3
By **Mimi**

TRAPHOUSE KING 1-3
KINGPIN KILLAZ 1-3
STREET KINGS 1&2
PAID IN BLOOD 1&2
CARTEL KILLAZ 1-3
DOPE GODS 1&2
By **Hood Rich**

THE STREETS ARE CALLING
By **Duquie Wilson**

STEADY MOBBN' 1-3
THE STREETS STAINED MY SOUL 1-3
By **Marcellus Allen**

WHO SHOT YA 1-3
SON OF A DOPE FIEND 1-4
HEAVEN GOT A GHETTO 1&2
SKI MASK MONEY 1&2
By **Renta**

GORILLAZ IN THE BAY 1-4
TEARS OF A GANGSTA 1/&2
3X KRAZY 1&2
STRAIGHT BEAST MODE 1&2
By **DE'KARI**

TRIGGADALE 1-3
MURDA WAS THE CASE 1-3
By **Elijah R. Freeman**

SLAUGHTER GANG 1-3
RUTHLESS HEART 1-3
By **Willie Slaughter**

GOD BLESS THE TRAPPERS 1-3
THESE SCANDALOUS STREETS 1-3
FEAR MY GANGSTA 1-5
THESE STREETS DON'T LOVE NOBODY 1-2
BURY ME A G 1-5
A GANGSTA'S EMPIRE 1-4
THE DOPEMAN'S BODYGAURD 1&2
THE REALEST KILLAZ 1-3
THE LAST OF THE OGS 1-3
By **Tranay Adams**

MARRIED TO A BOSS 1-3
By **Destiny Skai & Chris Green**

KINGZ OF THE GAME 1-7
CRIME BOSS 1-4
By **Playa Ray**

FUK SHYT
By **Blakk Diamond**

DON'T F#CK WITH MY HEART 1&2
By **Linnea**

ADDICTED TO THE DRAMA 1-3
IN THE ARM OF HIS BOSS
By **Jamila**

LOYALTY AIN'T PROMISED 1&2
By **Keith Williams**

YAYO 1-4
A SHOOTER'S AMBITION 1&2
BRED IN THE GAME
By **S. Allen**

TRAP GOD 1-3
RICH $AVAGE 1-3
MONEY IN THE GRAVE 1-3
CARTEL MONEY 1&2
By **Martell Troublesome Bolden**

FOREVER GANGSTA 1&2
GLOCKS ON SATIN SHEETS 1&2
By **Adrian Dulan**

TOE TAGZ 1-4
LEVELS TO THIS SHYT 1&2
IT'S JUST ME AND YOU
By **Ah'Million**

KINGPIN DREAMS 1-3
RAN OFF ON DA PLUG
By **Paper Boi Rari**

THE STREETS MADE ME 1-3
By **Larry D. Wright**

CONFESSIONS OF A GANGSTA 1-4
CONFESSIONS OF A JACKBOY 1-3
CONFESSIONS OF A HITMAN
CONFESSIONS OF A DOPE BOY
By **Nicholas Lock**

I'M NOTHING WITHOUT HIS LOVE
SINS OF A THUG
TO THE THUG I LOVED BEFORE
A GANGSTA SAVED XMAS
IN A HUSTLER I TRUST
By **Monet Dragun**

QUIET MONEY 1-3
THUG LIFE 1-3
EXTENDED CLIP 1&2
A GANGSTA'S PARADISE
By **Trai'Quan**

CAUGHT UP IN THE LIFE 1-3
THE STREETS NEVER LET GO 1-3
By **Robert Baptiste**

NEW TO THE GAME 1-3
MONEY, MURDER & MEMORIES 1-3
By **Malik D. Rice**

CREAM 2-3
THE STREETS WILL TALK
By **Yolanda Moore**

THE STREETS WILL NEVER CLOSE 1-3
By **K'ajji**

LIFE OF A SAVAGE 1-4
A GANGSTA'S QUR'AN 1-4
MURDA SEASON 1-3
GANGLAND CARTEL 1-3
CHI'RAQ GANGSTAS 1-4
KILLERS ON ELM STREET 1-3
JACK BOYZ N DA BRONX 1-3
A DOPEBOY'S DREAM 1-3
JACK BOYS VS DOPE BOYS 1-3
COKE GIRLZ
COKE BOYS
SOSA GANG 1&2
BRONX SAVAGES
BODYMORE KINGPINS
BLOOD OF A GOON
By **Romell Tukes**

CONCRETE KILLA 1-3
VICIOUS LOYALTY 1-3
BLOODY MONEY BAGS
By **Kingpen**

THE ULTIMATE SACRIFICE 1-6
KHADIFI
IF YOU CROSS ME ONCE 1-3
ANGEL 1-4
IN THE BLINK OF AN EYE
By **Anthony Fields**

THE LIFE OF A HOOD STAR
By **Ca$h & Rashia Wilson**

NIGHTMARES OF A HUSTLA 1-3
BLOOD AND GAMES 1&2
By **King Dream**

GHOST MOB
By **Stilloan Robinson**

HARD AND RUTHLESS 1&2
MOB TOWN 251
THE BILLIONAIRE BENTLEYS 1-3
REAL G'S MOVE IN SILENCE
By **Von Diesel**

MOB TIES 1-7
SOUL OF A HUSTLER, HEART OF A KILLER 1-3
GORILLAZ IN THE TRENCHES
OOPS CRY TOO 1&2
THE DAUGHTER OF A CARTEL BOSS
By **SayNoMore**

BODYMORE MURDERLAND 1-3
THE BIRTH OF A GANGSTER 1-4
By **Delmont Player**

FOR THE LOVE OF A BOSS 1&2
By **C. D. Blue**

KILLA KOUNTY 1-5
TENDER
By **Khufu**

MOBBED UP 1-4
THE BRICK MAN 1-5
THE COCAINE PRINCESS 1-10
STEPPERS 1-3
SUPER GREMLIN 1-4
A GANGSTA'S SON
By **King Rio**

MONEY GAME 1&2
By **Smoove Dolla**

A GANGSTA'S KARMA 1-5
By **FLAME**

KING OF THE TRENCHES 1-3
By **GHOST & TRANAY ADAMS**

BAD BITCHES WIT GUNZ 1&2
PROBLEM SOLVED
By "Christopher Diesel" Hornezes

QUEEN OF THE ZOO 1&2
By **Black Migo**

GRIMEY WAYS 1-3
BETRAYAL OF A G
By **Ray Vinci**

XMAS WITH AN ATL SHOOTER
By **Ca$h & Destiny Skai**

KING KILLA 1&2
By **Vincent "Vitto" Holloway**

BETRAYAL OF A THUG 1&2
By **Fre$h**

COUNTDOWN OF A KILLA 1&2
SEX, MURDER AND GOD 1&2
GUNS DOWN, BOTTOMS UP 1&2
By Lo-Life

THE MURDER QUEENS 1-7
By **Michael Gallon**

FOR THE LOVE OF BLOOD 1-4
By **Jamel Mitchell**

QUEEN OF NAPTOWN | KEITH CHANDLER

HOOD CONSIGLIERE 1&2
NO TIME FOR ERROR
By **Keese**

PROTÉGÉ OF A LEGEND 1,2&3
LOVE IN THE TRENCHES 1&2
By **Corey Robinson**

THE PLUG'S RUTHLESS DAUGHTER 1&2
By **Tony Daniels**

BORN IN THE GRAVE 1-3
CRIME PAYS
By **Self Made Tay**

MOAN IN MY MOUTH
By **XTASY**

TORN BETWEEN A GANGSTER AND A GENTLEMAN
By **J-BLUNT & Miss Kim**

LOYALTY IS EVERYTHING 1-3
CITY OF SMOKE 1-3
By **Molotti**

HERE TODAY GONE TOMORROW 1&2
By **Fly Rock**

WOMEN LIE MEN LIE 1-4
FIFTY SHADES OF SNOW 1-3
STACK BEFORE YOU SPLURGE
GIRLS FALL LIKE DOMINOES
NAÏVE TO THE STREETS
By **ROY MILLIGAN**

PILLOW PRINCESS
By **S. Hawkins**

THE BUTTERFLY MAFIA 1-3
SALUTE MY SAVAGERY 1&2
By **Fumiya Payne**

THE LANE 1&2
By Ken-Ken Spence

THE PUSSY TRAP 1-5
By **Nene Capri**

DIRTY DNA
By **Blaque**

SANCTIFIED AND HORNY
by **XTASY**

BOOKS BY LDP'S CEO, CA$H

TRUST IN NO MAN
TRUST IN NO MAN 2
TRUST IN NO MAN 3
BONDED BY BLOOD
SHORTY GOT A THUG
THUGS CRY
THUGS CRY 2
THUGS CRY 3
TRUST NO BITCH
TRUST NO BITCH 2
TRUST NO BITCH 3
TIL MY CASKET DROPS
RESTRAINING ORDER
RESTRAINING ORDER 2
IN LOVE WITH A CONVICT
LIFE OF A HOOD STAR
XMAS WITH AN ATL SHOOTER

www.ingramcontent.com/pod-product-compliance
Lightning Source LLC
Chambersburg PA
CBHW070518260626
47161CB00004B/1581